George is married with two grown sons. He is a retired technician in computer manufacturing and lives in Ayrshire. When not there, he can be found at his static caravan near the Solway Firth, looking directly out on to the Irish Sea, and if not, he will be in Canada with his older son and family. He was in the Royal Military Police (TA) for twenty years. Inspiration for *Clans* came from years of camping and trekking in Scotland and Canada.

George Horton

CLANS

Donated by the very generous & charming Keeth Gulliver brother of Jane Coles.

AUSTIN MACAULEY PUBLISHERS™

LONDON · CAMBRIDGE · NEW YORK · SHARJAH

A CIP catalogue record for this title is available from the British Library.

ISBN 9781528914888 (Paperback)
ISBN 9781528914895 (Hardback)
ISBN 9781528961042 (ePub e-book)

www.austinmacauley.com

First Published (2019)
Austin Macauley Publishers Ltd
25 Canada Square
Canary Wharf
London
E14 5LQ

Synopsis

This is the story of five cave-dwelling clans of humans who lived nine-thousand years ago in what would become Northern Europe. They were isolated from the rest of human kind by the vast European central plain and in their long clan memory, they had never encountered other people.

A warrior people from the south on a slaving expedition attacked them, many of the clans were killed. This attack was the start of many changes to the life of the clans and would eventually lead to a calendar, the beginning of counting, writing, and in the future, monuments of stone that still exist today. Another invention much in use in other parts of the world was the needle, this simple device would transform the life and health of the people.

Eventually, they will meet and join with the horse people of the eastern plain to the mutual benefit of all.

After adventures, they and the horse people will be aided by the Tufek, the forest people, and attack the slavers in a final battle.

The Clans

MOYAN, MOREE, BUREEN, RABEEL and MIZUKI.

The Moyan were the most northerly, about twelve miles to their south lived the Mizuki the most southerly of the five clans.

The population of the five clans was about three-hundred.

The people were peaceable and cooperated with each other in various enterprises usually involving hunting. Life was hard this far north, warfare was unknown. Sometimes around a fire, people speculated that there must be other clans far to the south, but in clan memory, they had always been alone. Their speculation on other clans was to prove correct.

The Vornay

A tribe of nomadic horse-men living in extended family groups loosely cooperating with each other, they were separated from the clans by a range of mountains cutting across the plain from north to south with the Vornay on the eastern side and the clans on the western side; neither people knew of each other's existence.

The Adnin

A people living on the great plain several hundred miles south of the five clans and the Vornay, they were slavers raiding the tribes to their south and east, more advanced than both the clans and the Vornay; they used pottery, metal, agriculture and lived in a town built from wood and stone.

They had found religion and made human sacrifices, and were ruled by a priest king.

The Tufek

A forest-living people west of the Adnin, and because of the difficult forest terrain and the Tufek's use of blow pipes and poison darts originally used to bring animals down out of the trees, they remained unconquered by Adnin.

Characters

The original names of these people have been lost in the mist of time.

Moyan

Fred	Used counting to find Midsummer Day.
June	Fred's wife.
Junior	Fred's Son.
Mike	Leader of the Moyan.
Ruby	Mike's wife.
Jake	A leader of the hunters.
Willy	Fred's best friend and a future hunter leader. Marries Alice of the Vornay
Ava	Daughter of Willy and Alice.
Rab	A hunter, the tallest and the keenest.
Jock	The youngest of the hunters. Leader of the expedition south… fair hair, fresh-faced.
Jim	Junior's best friend and on his expedition to the sea.
George	The flint knapper.
Sasha	Junior is keen on her.
Ella	Sasha's mother.
Luke	Fred's apprentice.
Ben	Fred's apprentice.
Alan	One of Junior's friends and on his expedition to the sea
Isla	would become Jock's wife.
Wally	One of Junior's friends and on his expedition to the sea.

Moree

Nearest clan to the Moyan.

Ash	Clan leader. Kick-starts the clans' 'enlightenment'.
Jean	Ash's wife. Discovers natural needles.
Barny	Junior's friend. On Jock's expedition south.
Duke	Junior's friend.
Nat	Junior's friend.
Benny	Junior's friend.
Tam	The flint knapper.

Bureen

The next nearest clan.

Murf	Leader.
Emily	His wife.
Brian	Friend of Junior.
Adam	Friend of Junior.
Terry	A hunter and in the expedition south.

Rabeel

The second furthest away.

Star	The leader.
Rab	A hunter.
Beks	In expedition south.
Karl	Friend of Junior.
Isla	Marries Jock.
Robin	A hunter.

Mizuki

The furthest away.

Ben	The leader.
Barry	Boy… orphaned.
Sam	Boy… orphaned.
Merz	The flint knapper.

Vornay

The horse people.

Buster	Leader of first expedition to the west plain.
Lilly	His wife.
Jude	His son, and on Jock's expedition sout
Alice	Buster's daughter. Marries Willy.
Blake	Buster's brother.
Poppy	Blake's wife.
Darren	A child.
Kai	Leader of advance party to the Vorna families.
John	Head of the senior Vornay families.

Adnin

Rufus	Priest king. Ruler of the town of Geyin.
Valious	Prime priest and second in command.
Oliver	Soldier.
Jacob	Soldier.
Harry	Soldier.
Charlie	Slave.
Noah	Slave.
Joe	Captured priest.
Jenny	Slave

Forest People.

The Tufek

Max	A village headman.
Davy	Escaped slave.
John	A village headman.
Hugh	Most senior headman.

Prologue

Nine-thousand years ago in Northern Europe, on a tree-covered escarpment, overlooking the Great European Plain, lived the five clans. Their home caves stretched out in a line along the escarpment. At the southern end, the escarpment gradually fell away until it reached an arm of the great sea.

Life for the people was hard and very short. In other climes, man was starting agriculture living in villages and towns making pottery, weaving, working with metal. But not here at this time and in this place, the humans for the most part lived in caves, their short lives had not changed much in generations, they communicated verbally and in sign language, a vestige left over from their ancestors.

Today, mankind (unfortunately) dominates all aspects of Mother Nature and planet Earth, his heavy hand has been felt everywhere.

Nine-thousand years ago, it was a different story, early man's imprint on the planet was negligible, as a result, plant and animal life blossomed, everywhere, the great herbivores of the plains lived in their tens of millions, the animals that preyed on them barely made a dent. Life in the seas and rivers was equally bountiful, the birds of the air flocked in unimaginable numbers.

In Northern Europe, man living in this seemingly bountiful planet, however, didn't find life easy, it was

one long battle to find enough to eat and to store food for the winter, there were many losers.

Part One

Chapter One
Spring Hunt

It was early spring and for the first time in weeks, the day was frost-free. Fred, this isn't his real name that has been lost in the sands of time, he was a hunter for the Moyan clan. He was typical of men of his time, just over five-feet tall, stoically built, different from his peers by a shock of red hair and a thin, barely visible red beard.

Fred and the other hunters, seven in all, came down the escarpment towards the great plain, their descent angled south in the hope of meeting the first of the great herds of plains' animals as they migrate north for the summer. As they descended towards the edge of the tree line, the only sound was the wind in the branches of the huge pine trees causing the upper branches to creak and groan, but at ground level, all was quiet. They reached the edge of the tree line, crawled out, and laid down gratefully in the sun and surveyed the plain and the herd below.

The herd of aurochs was small, numbering a few hundred, the forerunners of the huge numbers migrating up from the south.

In early spring, the grass was not as lush as it would be in a few weeks' time, but the aurochs looking huge in their shaggy winter coats would be thin under these coats and were eating on what grass there was, they had overwintered in the less harsh conditions further south and were eager to reach their summer pastures.

These animals, like the caribou, reindeer and bison, were non-migratory in the real sense, moving only a few hundred miles south to more sheltered forested areas.

* * * *

It had been a long winter in the caves, babies had been born, men, women and children had died, hunting was almost non-existent, the clan relied on their store of dried meat and fish, and their meagre store of roots and berries, now mostly rotten.

The supply of wood for the fires had lasted well, augmented by expeditions into the woods when weather allowed.

Winter weather severely curtailed the clan's activities leading to boredom and arguments. Only the strong leadership of Mike, their leader, kept the Moyan clan together.

* * * *

Many, many, many miles to the north of the clan's caves, far beyond the horizon were white ice peaks, the vestige of a glacier that had been slowly receding for hundreds of years. It helped feed the streams and rivers flowing south across the great plain. Far-far-far to the east, a chain of snow-capped mountains stretched north to south. The mountains were so far away that the clans didn't know of their existence, and if they did, these mountains were too far away to be explored, and to the south the great plain extended as far as the eye could see and seemingly went on forever.

Fred's best mate was Willy, he too was a hunter. They were of an age, about nineteen and like the rest of the clan at this time, would be lucky to reach thirty.

In their younger days, before the responsibilities of adulthood, they roamed the summer hills around the caves. Practising spear throwing, trapping small animals, occasionally, actually spearing or catching one, finding all the best places for edible roots, berries and tubers, trees to climb, rivers and streams to fish, visits to the inlet, an arm of the great sea to scrape salt and as puberty arrived, girls to ogle and chase, sometimes the chase wasn't too hard.

Fred already had a wife, June; a son, Fred Junior, about five; and the baby, Miss Fred.

Willy on the other hand with his jet-black hair, no beard, was a favourite with the girls. Not only the girls of the clan, the girls of all the clans. Being slightly built and just five feet tall, he was built to run, in future times, he would be described as fast as a whippet. As yet, he still had to find a mate. Willy had time for everyone, even the children, and with his easy smile, he was one of the most popular men across all the clans.

Willy moved over to Jake, the hunter leader, and pointing to a tree-lined gully worn down by a stream, said and sighed, "We can get a lot closer going down the stream."

Jake agreed, the hunters backed into the trees, turning right until they reached the stream and started to follow it down towards the edge of the plain. The stream, while not in spate, was heavy with spring run-off. Jake, the oldest and leader, was starting to show his age, his beard was showing grey and he seemed to have a persistent cough.

"Whose bright idea was this?" he said and sighed as he stumbled on slippery rocks for the umpteenth time and reaching out to grab a tree branch, he missed and fell painfully into the rocky streambed.

Fred and Willy looked at each other, and with the little sympathy of the young in unspoken agreement, realised that Jake wouldn't be the leader of the hunters for much longer as he was older, smaller and round-shouldered caused by a lifetime of hard work.

They continued their wet, cold, stumbling trek down the stream towards the plain and the herd; they had been on the go for five hours and knew that this was the easy part.

Twenty minutes later, the stream with a last hurrah tumbled twenty feet down a sheer rock face on to the great plain.

It was before midday, they were tired, cold and wet but at least the sun was shining, time for a rest, a warm-up and something to eat. The herd was almost in earshot, no orders were necessary, not a word was spoken, instead, they silently signed to each other.

Signing was an old-old way of communicating between individuals still in use but language was far more versatile and was increasing in complexity and now far more common.

They chewed on dried strips of meat later known as beef jerky and drank water from the stream. The dried meat was almost the last of the clan's reserves, if this hunt was unsuccessful, hunger would once again stalk the clan.

Willy pointed to a tor, a rocky outcrop in the plain about ten tens of paces away from them, he whispered and signed, "If we get there, we can plan the attack."

The tor was within a ten and another ten paces to the nearest group of aurochs, the hunters using the tumbling stream as cover, dropped silently down on to the plain, and on their bellies squirmed through the wet grass towards the outcrop and thanks to the prevailing winds, they arrived undetected.

Jake signed to Rab, the tallest hunter yet to have a beard. He had the best eye to spot an old or slightly injured animal (any injury other than slight would never have gotten this far). He crept up the tor to best observe the herd, and came back a few minutes later and took the hunters two at a time back up and singled out the target animal.

The hunters split in two and squirmed round the tor. Jake squirmed undetected a few paces ahead, slowly and silently got to his feet, unbelievably, the herd ignored him, no word or sign was necessary. The rest of the hunters slowly rose to their feet and quietly moved forward, eventually, an animal lifted its head, saw the danger, bellowed and took off. The rest of the herd like an outward going ripple in a pond followed.

Rab had chosen his target well. The animal was slow to move off and was hindered by animals overtaking it on all sides. The hunters raced towards their prey, spears at the ready. Fred and Willy tore past Jake with all the energy of hungry teenagers, and were within less than ten paces before losing their fire-hardened-tipped spears, their aim was true, one spear in its rump, another in its left side and as it twisted, jostled by other animals. It stumbled, allowing Rab and Jock, the youngest of the hunters to get even closer before losing their weapons. Jock's spear hit a telling strike to the side of the animal's neck while Rab's spear struck the top of it neck.

This had been the easy part of the hunt. An animal maddened with pain and losing blood would take off across the plain with the hunters hot on its heels and a lot of the time not very hot, the chase was brutal, unbroken ground sometimes marshy, sometimes stony, sometimes waist high grasses, stumbling into unseen holes.

Jumping or wading across streams. A broken leg was the end for a hunter and often even his life.

On a bad day, the prey animal could run for half a day before eventually it would tire, slow down and allow the hunters to catch up and finish the job, and then totally exhausted, they would simply lay down.

The hunters, the elite of the clan, took the 'lion's share' of food. Their needs took priority over the rest of the clan and why not, life for everyone in the clan life was hard but in the hunters, it was especially so, a hunter was in a prestigious position but this position was always all too short, but without them, the clan would not survive.

When an animal was killed, the followers came and helped. Ex-hunters now too old or injured to be in the hunting team and had been following the hunters. Their job was to assist in butchering the kill and help transport the meat and skins back to the clan caves, not an easy task with an animal weighing a quarter ton especially when the only tools available were made from flint, bone wood and hide. There was compensation, however, for all a much-prized delicacy, still warm heart, liver and kidneys.

* * * *

The auroch was unwilling to give up yet and although sorely wounded, galloped after the herd. The hunters whooped with joy as they raced to follow. This chase would not go on for a day or even hours.

The sun had barely moved before the beast slowed down enough for the hunters to catch up and finish the job. They approached the injured animal. It would be hard to judge who was the more exhausted, hunter or prey. Jake, the oldest, was on the verge of collapse, his breath coming in great shuddering waves, falling to his knees, he dug his spear into the ground in front of him and held on with both hands. The rest of the hunters were sympathetic. They all needed a rest.

Fred sat and then lay on the ground, his breathing only slightly less laboured than his leader. There was no need for urgency; the wounded animal was not going anywhere. It was still standing but even with its head down, could still be dangerous.

The frozen tableau lasted for many heartbeats until the hunters recovered and surrounded the animal and with a sign from Jake, advanced and killed the auroch; there was no thanking the great spirits for a successful hunt, no thanking the spirit of the animal for giving up itself to benefit man. Gods and spirits were still to influence the clans at this time.

Earlier, the followers up on the escarpment had watched events and started to make their way down even before the hunt had ended in the hope that they could share in the warm delicacies of the beast's innards. They carried flint axes, flint knives, bone hammers, wooden clubs and animal hides which they used in the task of cutting and dismembering. The bonus of this task was the still warm heart, liver and kidneys.

Everyone joined in on the bloody task of dismembering the animal into manageable sizes for transport back to the home caves.

The trek back was exhausting but uneventful. The spring sun was unusually warm and their loads heavy.

Jake called to young Jock, "Run on ahead and start the preparations for our arrival."

Young Jock with the fresh face of a youth, fair-haired, barely thirteen and quite possibly still growing, ran on ahead to warn the clan and start the celebration for the first successful hunt of the season. As the most junior of the hunters, he was glad to have a bit of responsibility and independence, he ran and ran. When he reached home, he went straight to Mike's wife, Ruby. She was heavily pregnant but in the lives of the people, pregnancy was no bar to heavy work. Often a woman would give birth and an hour later, with her new-born wrapped in her furs, would be back at work. This environment took a heavy toll on women and was one of the long lists of conditions that contributed to their short lifespan.

Ruby immediately organised the women to damp down the fire pits, they were already burning in anticipation of a successful hunt. Other fires lit, stones heated, skins full of water carefully heated over open flames. The water absorbing the heat, preventing damage to the skins and monitored by older girls and woe betide them if they allowed the flames to burn through the skins. The very last of the dried meat softened and added to the last of the roots, berries and tubers left after the winter and heated in the skins.

When the teams arrived with their life bounty, it was already dark, stars shone, the moon helped but in early spring, it was cold, the people wrapped themselves in their furs.

The light of the fires outside the caves gave enough light to prepare the last of the winter supplies. But it would be the next day before the first of the meat would be ready and with their much-diminished supplies, the clan went to bed that night fed but still hungry, however, the fire pits would provide food for days and days.

In the caves, the only light was from wicks of twisted animal hair soaked in fat and floating in natural and man-made hollows in the rock. The light was minimal and the smell abysmal but in pitch-blackness, it was better than nothing and as the saying goes, 'in the land of the blind, the one-eyed man is king'.

Chapter Two
Home Caves

The Moyans' home was five caves of various sizes set in a vertical cliff of basalt and limestone rock half way up the escarpment. Four of the caves were interconnected caused by water erosion aeons ago; the larger fifth cave was used for storage; mainly, dried meat, salt and wood. Without a huge supply of wood for the fires, there would be no clans.

Each family has their own allocated space in the system, low man-made stonewalls within the caves gave a measure of privacy, where their few possessions and furs were kept, the walls helped divert draughts. Each family had a hearth, which in winter burned continuously. These smoky, cold, damp, smelly, unhygienic conditions were another circumstance that contributed to the short life span of the people.

Another contributor was vermin, their hair and fur wraps infested to an extent that itching and scratching was just part of everyday life, and in the summer down on the plain, blood-sucking insects only kept partially at bay with smoky fires.

Outside the caves was a flat area beaten down by generations of feet. The only features were a dead pine tree, its branches removed long ago for firewood and now a solitary finger of wood pointing to the sky. In this story, it will be called the lonesome pine; another feature was a large boulder too big to be removed. It had a promontory near the top that always reminded hunter Fred of his late mother-in-law's hooked nose. He was, of course, not brave enough to compare the likeness. The other features were the clan's fire pits and a stream running down to the great plain. Further down the escarpment were their middens, and in a gully to the right of the middens and fed by another stream were the clan's latrines and even further on down was the clan's graveyard.

The graves were marked with a small pile of stones. People liked to remember their departed loved ones and sometimes arranged these small stone cairns in a certain way. The cairns were not just a remembrance to the people of the clans, importantly, they were also an indicator where not to dig a new grave.

Today, we remember our dead in a much grander fashion.

In winter when the ground was too hard to dig, and when most of the deaths took place, the body would be cremated, and in a bad winter, this caused a shortage of wood.

The morning after the hunt, everyone was up early. Today, they would for the first time in months, eat freshly cooked meat, tenderised by a night in the fire pits. Everyone settled down to eat the meat and the very last of the tubers. This was one of the occasions that the clan ate together, mostly, a woman cooked for her family.

* * * *

The next day, the sun shone with only a few light clouds racing across the sky. The wind at ground level was light; everyone could feel its warmth on their face.

Jake, perhaps, aware of his precarious position as leader of the hunters decided that there should be another hunt.

No one wanted to go so soon after the first hunt. Fred and Willy were the most outspoken and argued with Jake, the rest of the hunters agreed with Fred and Willy but were less outspoken, especially Jock, who was the youngest and newest of the hunters and didn't want to jeopardise his prestigious position in the group. This argument like all arguments within the clan ended at Mike's door.

Jake, having made the decision to hunt the next day, was adamant, as he didn't want to lose face by being overruled by his team. Fred and Willy, on the opposition side, pointed out that the herd would be long gone by now and there had been no sign of the great herds migrating up from the south.

Mike as usual had to make peace with everyone and although he secretly agreed with the majority, he couldn't let Jake's authority be undermined. He came down on Jake's side, and said to Fred and Willy and the rest of the hunters, "You may well be right, it is a bit early to mount another hunt but Jake is your leader and if there is to be another hunt today, so be it."

The mumps and moans from the hunters increased. Mike raised his hands and threw a crumb of comfort to the majority by saying, "The weather is fine for now, in a few days' time the frosts or rains may be back. Jake is right, so make the best of it while you can when the weather is good."

And so, the next day in the morning light, the hunters reluctantly gathered together and set off for the plain.

Moving straight down, they were there in two hours, and when they came out of the trees at the bottom of the escarpment, the herd had moved on and were nowhere to be seen. But in the distance, the hunters spotted a single cow and her offspring. She must have stumbled in a hole and broken her leg.

Jake whooped with delight at the ease of this hunt. He, no doubt, felt justified in ordering a second hunt so soon, and with the kill being so close to home and the hunters still fresh, there was going to be nothing left for the scavengers, every bit of the animal meat bone and sinew would be dissected and transported home.

In the late afternoon, the triumphant return of the hunters and followers was sweetened with the sight of dozens and dozens of fish gutted and drying on rocks. The women had been down to the river and found the fish were running upstream to spawn. There was no need to fish, it was sufficient to wade in the water, and with their woven reed baskets, scoop them out and throw them on to the bank and collected by children.

Fred had barely arrived in the Moyan clan's communal space outside the caves when an excited Fred Junior came running up to tell his father of his and his friend's first ever kill.

"We killed a deer," Junior announced proudly.

While they were roaming the hills, they came across deer's spoor and decided to set a noose trap. They set it, left it and went further up the mountain to look for edible plants, roots and tubers and early flowers. This operation too was successful in a small glen protected by trees and nourished by a stream and in the soft loom was a bounty of wild onion, roots, tubers and edible plants, too early in the year to be collected but some were lifted anyway. On their way back, a young fallow deer was caught in their trap.

It had been a long time since there was such an abundance of food so early on in the year.

Mike the leader of Fred's clan was tall for a man of his time, nearly five feet five but not as muscular as some, his lighter frame made him fast and he was the very best of the hunters and a natural hunter leader and under his leadership, the Moyan clan had prospered.

The old clan leader, Solegeb, had died three winters ago. Mike was everyone's choice as leader, but in the next three years, the clan had suffered, in part to severe winters but also in part to Jake, the new leader of the hunters and his poorer abilities.

Mike's clan numbered less than fifty, not that he knew that as he couldn't count. The winter had been a hard one. The stored food had barely lasted, the cold had taken its toll among the young and old, eight members of the clan had not survived and Mike knew intuitively that the survival of the clan and that of the neighbouring clans was on co-operation and working together especially in the great autumn hunt.

Thus, as the hunters left for their second hunt, he and Yan, the medicine man, visited the caves of their nearest neighbours, the Moree, ostensibly to arrange trade and talk about the great summer festival when all the clans met on the great plain and feasted and competed in the games. The real reason for the visit was to find out how the Moree had fared over the winter.

In fact, they had fared less well than the Moyan. They were yet to make their first kill of the spring, things were dire but courtesy demanded the two men from the Moyan be treated as honoured guests and fed appropriately.

On arrival back with the clan, Mike was astounded to find so much food, more than enough for the clan and his thoughts turned to the Moree, his immediate selfless action showed why man has been raised above the animals. He immediately prepared to transport meat, fish

28

and, and much to Junior's disappointment, the young fallow deer to the Moree.

The next morning, he accompanied men carrying these life-saving gifts, and on arrival at his nearest neighbours, wise beyond his years, he played down the gifts, saying and signing the truth that we have just been very lucky and one day, the Moree might return the complement.

While Mike and the men were taking food to Moree, Fred found that for once in his life, he was at a loose end with a full stomach and nothing much to do. Jane was busy with the baby, Junior and friends were off learning how to knap flint with George, the flint knapper.

Chapter Three
Calendar

It was a sunny spring midmorning and Fred was sitting outside his cave, enjoying the Stone Age herbal equivalent of a piña colada and watching the world go by.

In front of him was the cleared flat meeting ground where the clan activities took place. A hundred paces to his right was the beginning of the tree-covered escarpment. The only features were the lonesome pine and the rock with the nose and the fire pits.

The spring sun cast the shadow of the lonesome pine to the left of the 'nose' and as the minutes passed and with nothing much else to do, he noticed the shadow had moved towards the rock and after a few minutes, just touched the bottom of the rock before moving on to the right.

The life of the clan, however, continued mostly centred on gathering food, processing animal hide and bone to make everything from wraps (clothes) to bedding, to ropes to flint knapping, to recounting the history of the people to storytelling and teaching the children.

This spring was a good time, food became easier to find, hunt fish or trap and after a hard winter, everyone was happier and looking forward to warm bountiful summer.

Two weeks later at the beginning of June, Fred was once again at a bit of a loose end, and enjoying a piña colada and watching the world go by. Again, he noticed the shadow of the lonesome pine as it moved towards the boulder but this time the shadow moving from left to right, it fell short of it.

Everyone knew that shadows were shorter in the summer, and longer in the winter and shorter in the middle of the day and longer in the morning and evening, but with their limited vocabulary, holding a discussion on the properties of shadows cast by the sun was way down the list of the clan's priorities. The main topic of signing and talking was always food as hunger was never far away.

Fred, in noticing that the shadow of the lonesome pine was shorter than a few days before, had joined the first two dots in a puzzle that would change the lives of the clans. The conscious part of his brain didn't know this but, that marvellous and much underestimated and least understood part of the human brain, the sub-conscious, did.

How many so-called modern humans with all our trials and tribulations have gone to bed with a troubling problem unresolved only to wake up the next morning to find a solution had presented itself, it was the same with Fred. He didn't know why the change in shadow length was significant. He didn't even know what significant meant but his subconscious told him that the changes in the length of the lonesome pines shadow were somehow important.

Fred, as his entire race at this time, had one advantage over modern man, he had a terrific memory. Without the written word, how else could stories, histories, information be passed on to the next generation.

Fred, the hunter, Fred, the husband, Fred, the father, kept an eye on the shadows cast by the lonesome pine, and as the shadows crept ever shorter and further away from the 'nose' and as the year crept on towards midsummer, he remembered the shadow's mark on the various stones littering the clan's meeting place.

Then it happened, shortly after midsummer, the shadow of the lonesome pine started to lengthen and creep back towards the 'nose' and Fred realised that the summer was on the wane. He had joined the third dot to the puzzle. He had discovered midsummer's day and with that great memory of his, he went back to the spot in the clan's meeting place and placed a flat rock marking that place, and he remembered that midsummer coincided with a new moon. Fred marked his midsummer new moon rock with a flint hammer making a single line and a single curve, which came to mean something for a word he already knew, that word was for the figure one and so Fred started on the road to writing and counting.

* * * *

Fast forward to the twenty-first century in South America, there lived and still does today, a tribe, who until fairly recently, lived in isolation, shunning contact with the rest of the world. They were peaceful, known about, but no outsider had lived with them, studied them or learned their language. It was only when loggers moved onto their land that a plea for help allowed outsiders to live with them, one of their discoveries was that in their language, they had words for numbers one to ten, above that, they only had one word, which meant more than ten.

"And so how many fish did you catch today?"

"I caught seven."

"Very good."

"How many arrows did you make today?"

"Why? I made more than ten."

It is a fair bet that nine-thousand years ago, early man living in caves used the same system for counting.

Chapter Four
Summer Festival Enlightenment

With the arrival of high summer, the clans started to prepare for the summer festival.

It was held on the great plain below the escarpment and lasted for five days, during which there was much eating and indulging in a rare herb with hallucinating properties much favoured by older men.

Younger men, practically boys, were more concerned with the opposite sex, liaisons made and with negotiations with the clan chiefs, some young men and women moved to a different clan.

Children toys shown, judged and exchanged. Children ran in races with toys as prizes, flint knapper's latest tools shown, judged and exchanged. Hunters competed in spear throwing, wrestling and tall stories. Processed animal skins shown and judgements made on the finish and quality. The latest design for fur wraps shown and judged. But, if truth known, clothing design had not changed much in generations.

For the women of the clans, this was the best of times. Tradition had it that for one day each, a clan fed the other clans, therefore, for four days, the women were relieved of the drudgery of feeding their families. For them, this was a wonderful break and a great exercise in logistics, co-operation and an excuse to criticise quietly other woman's culinary and organisational efforts.

This summer festival would turn out to be the most important event in the history of the five clans. It was the start of their 'enlightenment', they were about to start catching-up with other people in other places in the world.

The clan Moree provided the greatest surprise of the festival.

Their chief, Ash and his wife, Jean, were the hit of the event. First, Ash and his men erected the biggest tent ever seen. It was huge compared to the modest shelters dotted about the plain. People were able to stand up inside. Everyone came to gape at this huge structure, supported by stout wooden poles and even had flaps at the entrance to keep out the weather and a central hearth. The smoke from its fire kept down the biting insects to a minimum. Close examination showed that it comprised of many bison skins sewn together; no one had ever seen anything like it. The seams were closely stitched in a way never seen before.

The next showstopper was when Ash and Jean went into their new tent and changed out of their summer furs and leather wraps into what today would be seen as clothes. They wore jerkins made of the supplest of leather. Ash's jerkin was sleeveless but Jean's had sleeves down to her wrists. The sleeves were rectangles of leather stitched to form a tube and stitched to the jerkin at the shoulders. They both wore leggings tied at the waist and the loose leggings criss-crossed with thin strips of leather.

It was Jean who made the discovery. One day when she was preparing meat, she found a splintered bone, sharp at one end with a hole at the other end she had found a natural needle. Then she made the next leap. Using stretched animal sinew as a thread, she sewed two pieces of fur skin together and changed the world of the clans forever.

Improvements quickly followed, Tam, the Moree flint knapper, split and ground suitable bones, and learned how to drill out the eye by patiently digging it out with a slither of flint. He became so good at making needles that he could make ten a day. Boys searched through the middens for suitable bones and with flints, splintered and broke them down for Tam. Meanwhile, Jean, already used to using sinew, washed and stretched it to make a passable thread or cord.

It says much of the peaceable people that Jean gave the woman of the other clans all of her spare needles. It took some persuading to stop them all rushing off there and then to their home caves to practice this new technology, while Tam was besieged by the other flint knappers and was soon giving practical lessons in the art of needle manufacture.

It was the invention of the needle that brought about a major change in the lives and health of the clans over the next few years. The summer camps, set out on the plain became ever more sophisticated. Three summer festivals later, people were becoming reluctant to go back to cold, dark, wet, smelly caves when they could be in warm, light, dry and just a wee bit smelly tent.

The invention of the needle made another big impact on the clans. Furs and leather could be cut and sewn in ways, impossible before, leading to increased improvements in the tanning of leather and the gradual introduction to all of what would become clothes.

The children were responsible for the next leap forward to the health and well-being of the clans. During a hot summer festival day, they were playing by one of the streams and came across a bed of clay washed out by the spring floods and started making crude animals with twigs for legs. Eventually getting bored, they wandered off leaving them on the bank, unknowing that the sun would dry out and harden the clay.

A few days later, Emily of the Bureen found them and picking a toy up, found it to be hard but crumpled easily. Lying a few feet away was a ball of clay abandoned by a child. It had a hollow scooped out of the top made with little fingers; she stooped, picked it up and had an idea. She went to the stream and scooped up water, looked at it, the water held. She put the clay ball to her lips and sipped and she joined most of the rest of the human race that were using clay pots and platters.

The clan's utensils for eating and cooking were mainly animal skins, specially made sticks to move hot stones used to heat water, sticks to dig out meat that had been wrapped in leaves placed on hot coals and buried in the ground and wooden vessels. These bowls were hard to make and very labour intensive. Unknown to the clans, the bowls harboured a myriad of germs and bacteria and strong as the people's constitution was, these eating bowls were the cause of much of the clan's ailments and deaths especially among the very young.

Emily enlisted the help of the children of her clan, the Bureen, and together they started to shape and make pots, bowls and platters, leaving them in the sun to dry. At first, these new eating implements were too fragile to be practicable. Later, placing them by a fire helped but not by much, someone in frustration threw a broken bowl on to the fire. Later when the broken piece was retrieved, it proved hard and almost useable, soon clay utensils were being treated in a similar way as cooking meat; buried on a bed of hot coals. Improvements followed as the people found that the hotter and the longer the pots were in the coals, the harder was the result.

In the time to scrape one wooden bowl, dozens of clay pots could be made in any shape or size. Brittle and short lived as they were, they soon become the norm for the clan to eat out of. If a bowl or platter broke, there were plenty more to replace it and as wooden bowls fell out of favour, the health of the people improved.

There was another benefit to clay over wood. It wasn't practicable for a family or indeed a clan to manufacture pottery. All the clans co-operated to produce it, soon men from different clans worked together to produce for all, thus the seeds of nationhood started to germinate.

Months after clay pots and plates became the norm, Fred's wife, June, while tidying up their space in the cave and complaining about her husband and sons' untidy habits, came across their old wooden food bowl. Looking inside, she did not like the look of the growths on the inner surfaces and with one sniff, was disgusted at the smell, she immediately consigned the bowl to the nearest fire.

Chapter Five
The Great Hunt

After the great summer meetings, the clans started to prepare for the great hunt of the year. The plains' animals would soon be gathering for their migration to the south. This was the time when all the clans united to make as many kills as possible to store and dry the meat for the hard times to come.

There was a problem however; the clans didn't have a calendar. They knew that summer was ending. On the other hand, the plains' animals danced to a different tune, in the modern calendar, in the second or third week of October, the great herds started their southward migration.

Without a calendar, the clans had to guess when to move out on to the plain, spread out and wait for the herds to start their migration. They also needed to scout and find out the route a herd would be taking this year and then prepare the traps and corrals.

The problem was the weather, if the summer was cold and wet, the hunters sometimes thought the year was further on than it was. As a consequence, they moved out on to the plain too early resulting in a miserable time, living out in the open, food running short, cold and wet, augmenting their diet with small animals who seemed to be expert in avoiding their traps, tempers becoming short and arguments breaking out.

Worse was when the autumn weather was fine and warm. An 'Indian summer'. If the hunters delayed going out on to the plain, thinking it was late summer and not autumn, they had little time to prepare for the arrival of the herds, resulting in a hungry winter and if they delayed too long and missed the annual migrations altogether, starvation and death stalked the clans. What was needed was a calendar and a datum point to start it off. Fred already had a datum point, midsummer day and with instinct guided by his subconscious, every new moon, he placed and marked a flat rock indicating the sun's shadow and with increasing length, the shadow reached the nose and then reached beyond it.

* * * *

When it was time for the great hunt in October, the hunters could be away for weeks, Fred, realising the importance of knowing when the herds started their migration, enlisted the help of Junior.

"Every day mark the furthest reach of the lonesome pine's shadow and mark it with a rock."

Junior's "Yes, dad," lacked enthusiasm.

"And look after your mum and your sister."

"Yes, dad."

The hunt was started by each clan sending out hunters to find and track the herds. Willy, Rab and young Jock represented the Moyan, they met up with the other hunters and an age-old plan put into action. They split up and went in search of the herds. Every third morning, a runner would go back to his clan with an update which was passed on to the other clans. In a bad year, this could go on for weeks until the herds started their annual southern migrations. Once started, a plan of action was made, which herd was to be targeted? Preferably, the route closest to the caves and the size of the herd when a huge herd sometimes close to a million were forced to stampede, the crush and injuries would be enough to feed the clans all through the winter.

A herd of bison on this occasion chose the western route closest to the clan caves; the herd was huge, many miles long and wide. It would have to pass between the many rocky outcrops of tors and with strategically placed brush fires, set by the hunters, the nervous herd became more compact which made them even more nervous, choke points were created along the route, and the scene was set for the carnage of the bison and the continued existence of the clans.

Every able-bodied man, woman and child were on the plain before the herd approached the choke points and as many holes as possible, most just a foot deep, were dug.

Warily, the first of the herd approached the first choke point, suddenly rising from the grass, over a hundred men and woman on both sides of the huge herd, started shouting, screaming, waving arms and sticks. The herd spread over many, many paces wide, shied away from its edges becoming even more crowded. The two lines of people slowly started to move towards each other, the beasts became more and more crowded with each other and the stampede of the frightened animals began, the herd was so huge, it split in several places and became running rivers of brown and black animals.

One river of animals ran, as hoped for by the clans, between the several tors, some stumbling in the prepared holes resulting in painful broken legs. Their maddened painful cries only made matters worse. The majority of the animals, however, went through the first choke point, and would have spread out, if not for the two lines of men and women shouting and screaming, directing the animals to the second choke point. There a similar fate awaited them. The herd took more than a day to pass, the vast majority continuing south to warmer climes.

The scene left to the modern human was a scene from hell. But to the clans, it was a scene of salvation, hundreds of animals most still alive in great pain and some trying pitifully to follow the herd, the bellowing and screaming even effected the clans who now had the gruesome job of killing and preparing their kills for transport back to the home caves, a process that took weeks.

It was through this delay in processing the meat that the clan found out that the longer the meat was stored, the more tender it had become before eaten, smoked and stored.

When Fred got back from the great hunt, the whole clan was busy with preparing and storing the kills before winter set in. And it was some time before Fred was able to catch up with Junior and when he did, he found that eight days after he left, a runner came and called out the rest of the clan.

Chapter Six
Calendar Develops

Junior had recorded the position of the new moon and the position of the lone pines shadow on the meeting ground. Later, Fred realised that they had pinpointed the start of the great herd's southern migration.

In the weeks that followed, Fred, guided by his subconscious but increasingly by the realisation that something important was happening, monitored and recorded on flat stones, the advancing shadow of the lonesome pine.

In December, shortly after midwinter's day, the shadows started to shorten. Thus, Fred had discovered the shortest day of the year and the march to spring and summer, he marked a flat stone accordingly.

There was no written word for numbers. Fred soon was fed up, adding an extra stroke to each new flat rock and because he was a clever and resourceful man, he invented written symbols for the oral numbers one to ten. Therefore, Fred was the first man in his world to write down symbols that would one day become words for numbers.

Another milestone came the following March, the clan's oral and Fred's symbols and numbering system had reached ten and was all used up and yet the increasingly shortening shadows had not reached the midsummer point with its longest day.

The first hunt of spring again took Fred away. Jake the hunter leader had joined the followers. He had become quite breathless and had lost a lot of weight. No one knew what was wrong with him but everyone knew that his time with the followers would be short as indeed his time in this world would also be short, but the people of the clan looked after their own.

With Fred away, Junior took over the roll. The next new moon in April, Junior, as advised by Fred, used the symbol for ten followed by the symbol for one and again on Fred's return, between them they established the actual day that the herds returned. By June, Fred used the word for ten and the symbol for three to mark the progress of the full moon and the lengthening daylight as the world turned towards midsummer.

The life of the clans continued, babies were born, some died. Old people became infirm or had failing vision. Families looked after each other and helped other families in need.

With the successes of the spring hunts, the pressure on the hunters lessened, and Fred and now Junior were able to continue their observations.

One day as the two Fred's were watching the lonesome pine's shadow creep ever to their right, Mike appeared and asked what was going on.

Fred at first was reluctant to give anything away until he was more sure of his facts and after all, knowledge was power but, Junior, awed by being addressed by the leader of the clan and imbibed with all the innocence of youth, spilled the beans. He explained how the shadows became shorter as the summer wore on and how his dad had found the day when the year turned and headed towards autumn and winter. Mike wasn't impressed until he found that Junior, in the absence of his father, had discovered the day the herds had started their southern migration, it was as Junior explained, "Four new moons and eight days after the longest summer day."

Mike was amazed.

"Can you really tell when the great herds start to go south for the winter?"

Fred said, "I would like more time to see if they do it at the same time next year but yes, I think we can and while I was away in the first spring hunt, Junior here recorded the day that the herds returned."

Mike went away with much to think about, and that evening, he, Yan the medicine man and few of the senior men of the clan met by a fire and Mike told them what he had found out about the mystery of the sun's movements. He then outlined his plans for the two Freds, and after much signing and talking, it was agreed.

In the morning, Mike summoned Fred and told him of his plans, he, Fred and his son would be relieved of their duties and were to concentrate on understanding the heavens, the sun and the moon. It would be their job to let the clans know when it was time to go on to the plain and prepare for either the arrival or departure of the herds.

The two would be provided with anything they needed.

In reality at that moment in the clan's life, Fred's absence from the hunt would not be missed. Under the leadership of Willy, the new leader, hunting had been more successful and there were teenagers waiting in the wings to take Fred's place.

Part Two

Chapter Seven
The Tufek and the Adnin

Meanwhile, many, many miles south, the great plain started to give way to an even greater plain, more like a savannah, hills ranged west, south and east.

The Tufek People lived in the forest to the west. They lived in dozens of hutted villages carved out of the forest and like the northern clans, co-operated with each other and were peaceable. They fished, gathered fruits, berries and edible roots. They hunted forest animals using blowpipes and darts tipped in poison derived from flowers, a diluted form was addictive and popular.

There were other people living on the savannah, the Adnin. They had moved from huts and were now building in wood and stone. They used pottery and had discovered how to use metal, and were farmers.

Improved metal tools allowed them to build their wood and stone town even bigger, which, of course, was highly labour-intensive. Other southern plains tribes were conquered and enslaved to provide the labour.

The Adnin had also found religion.

Nine-thousand years later, the history of this planet from that day to this has shown that religion begets war and war always begets slavery and death.

Rufus the priest/king, having subdued his neighbouring tribes to the south, now turned his attention to the Tufek, the forest people. His soldiers, always accompanied by priests, were dispatched to subdue these forest heathens.

The attacks on the forest tribes were initially successful with several villages burned to the ground and prisoners taken as slaves, however, the forest clans were at home in their forest and the plains people were not. The last two attacks into the forest were a disaster. None of his soldiers and accompanied priests returned.

The Tufek had used a concentrated version of the poison for their darts to defend themselves, the dense forest undergrowth made ambush easy and the Tufek soon learned that darts bounced of chest plates but not off necks or legs and no matter where the dart entered, as long as it broke the skin, the results were the same.

Initially, the poison caused unconsciousness with the soldiers killed with spears where they lay, something the Tufek found difficult. The problem solved by an increase in potency of the poison but not before accidents in distilling caused a few deaths among them.

Rufus was humiliated in the eyes of his people and swore revenge on the forest heathens. He summoned Valious, his chief priest, and ordered him to take an even bigger expedition into the forest to subdue the Tufek.

Rufus had a secondary reason for sending Valious. He had for some time been suspicious of him and his desire to be more than second in command and not for the first time, Rufus took steps to remove potential threats to his kingship, and so, Valious led the most powerful army ever mounted by the Adnin. Some one-hundred soldiers, priests and slaves left their city and moved through the fields towards the forest. Rufus's propaganda machine had been at work, most of the people of the city turned out to wave them off, their farewell to the soldiers and priests was on the surface genuine but it was a bit muted. The ordinary people of the city did not live the lives of the political elite, they didn't own slaves. They were for the exclusive use of Rufus and his entourage.

The Adnin called their city Geyin, in fact, it wasn't a city proper, more like a small town but bigger than a village, most of the populace found life hard.

The priests occasionally took a daughter and no matter the protests, she was never seen again; in fact, loud protests by grief-stricken families ended in a night visit, and the families themselves would disappear.

The forest to the west of Geyin was a two-days' march. The weather was good, the going easy; slaves carried the supplies.

Rufus ordered that Tufek slaves be sacrificed on the high altar to ensure the success of his latest attack on the forest people.

Valious was probably one of the few who understood the perils of this attack. The majority of his soldiers were ignorant of the failure of the last two missions into the forest.

The soldiers that did know of the failures knew the penalty for careless talk and the spreading of lies.

The army approaching the forest did not go unnoticed, the word went out and the people retreated further into the forest, leaving a few men as bait, who allowed themselves to be seen thus enticing the Adnin column in the direction they wanted and towards a prepared ambush. The soldiers and priests had little experience in battle. For generations, their only action had been raids on unarmed plains villages and in recent years, the raids were rare. The villages to the south of the Adnin were either emptied, the people moving further south away from the slavers or they had been captured and enslaved.

The soldiers were led on to a well-worn game trail which led down to a wide shallow river, the same river that supplied their town and watered their fields. On the other side of the river, thirty Tufek shouted obscenities and exposed themselves to the gathering Adnin.

Valious rightly suspected a trap and decided not to react. Instead, he camped by the river for the night.

The Tufek did not attack directly during the night but there are ways to attack indirectly. They had gambled that the soldiers would camp by the river and the site chosen for their attack. Nearby were several nests of biting forest ants.

The Adnin were spending an uncomfortable and sleepless night, unused to the strange forest noises, flying insects and crawling things kept everyone awake but worse was to come.

Just before dawn, a few paces into the jungle, the Tufek started to dig into the ant nests dropping in hot coals even urinating into them, the enraged ants poured out and sensing the body heat of the Adnin, converged on to the beach.

Soldiers lying uncomfortably in the sand, found ants crawling over them, and were being bitten on face and hands by the angry ants, in reality, less than half were being bitten but word and panic spread like wildfire. Every one took to the water; most leaving weapons and armour abandoned on the beach.

As a misty dawn rose over the river, the forest people poured on to the beach recently vacated by their enemy who hardly noticed. They were too busy washing and ducking under the water trying to wash off real and imaginary ants. Some of the Tufek collected weapons and metal armour. The rest raised their blowpipes and sent streams of poison darts into the Adnin. The concentrated poison took effect in just a few tens of heartbeats, and soldiers, priests and slaves alike started to stagger sway and fall. Valious, wakened to the danger, screamed to his men to attack, only a few responded and as they waded to the shore, they were cut down with their own weapons. Further out, the Adnin saw the carnage to their brethren nearer the shore turned and tried to reach the far shore, a mere hundred paces away. Within twenty paces of the shore, scores of Tufek stepped out of the forest, walked calmly to the water's edge and finished the job; revenge for all the killings, taking of slaves and burning of villages was complete.

A full moon later, it became apparent that Valious and his army were not coming back. Such a huge loss soon became public knowledge and the loss of face brought down on Rufus again by the forest tribes brought him to edge of insanity with rage. He now didn't just sacrifice slaves, he started to sacrifice some of his own people. The citizens of the city of Geyin lived in fear.

In the twisted mind of Rufus, there was an underlying layer of cunning. His desire to be king was paramount, he elected to divert attention to his shortcomings and mistakes and go after another enemy, but where? The forest to the west was now out of the question, the great plain to the south and east was all but emptied by his army that only left the north, he circulated stories of northern heathens who did not believe in him, a true God. They were cannibals and needed to be attacked and killed before they came down in their hordes and destroyed their city.

However, his cunning caused him to be careful. He sent scouts north, forty men accompanied by two priests and fifteen slaves, they were not to attack any people they found, their objective was to capture a few and bring them back to Rufus for interrogation.

Day after day, week after week, they journeyed north. When they reached the mountains east of the clan's caves, they split up, one party turning on to the plain east of the mountains while the other party travelled on the plain west of the mountains.

Chapter Eight
Expedition to the Sea

One bright July day while Fred was still thinking of an action plan to forecast the migration of the plain's animals, Junior appeared and asked to be excused. The rest of his gang wanted to go on an expedition not just down to the river but down to the sea miles away which meant they would be away possibly for five or six nights.

Fred looked fondly at his son, still a boy, nearly a man. He was already taller than his dad, he had the fair hair and blue eyes of his mum.

Fred signed and said, "You already go down to the sea to collect salt, that's you and your friend's job."

"No, not that sea, the big sea. Alan's dad said when he was a boy, he and his friends went to where our sea was joined by a huge sea where you can look in every direction and there is nothing but water."

Fred smiled and said something that in the future would be repeated a billion times, "All right, as long as it's okay with your mother."

Junior and his best mate, Jim, and two of their friends, Wally and Alan, gathered the few possessions they owned; sleeping furs, a few flint knives, a stone hammer and wrapped up in leaves, dried meat jerky donated by the boys' mothers. They were about to leave when Mike and Yan appeared, the boys were over-awed and a bit frightened. As the men approached, Alan said, "Will they let us go? We haven't done anything wrong."

Mike stopped in front of the boys, smiled at their concern and with his full height of five feet five (nearly), towering above them, "I hear you are going on an expedition to the sea, but have you forgotten something? How will you light your fire at night and keep the wild animals away?"

The boys were dismayed. All their lives in the clan's home, there had always been fires, summer and winter, especially in winter, there always was fire.

Yan came forward and gave Alan an animal horn. It was filled with soft moss and was warm to the touch, inside were glowing coals. "Look after this, check the coals regularly and don't let them go out, here is a pouch with more coals and dried moss, here let me show you what to do."

Alan was impressed, a horn of hot coals is what the hunters took with them on the great autumn hunts.

The following morning and much to the embarrassment of the boys, most of the clan turned out to see them off and off they went, a few miles along the side of the escarpment straight to the nearest clan, the home of the Moree, and waiting for them, their friends, Barny, Nat and Duke. Further embarrassment followed as the Moree turned out to see the boys off, they went straight to the home of the clan Bureen and there waiting for them, Terry Adam and Brian. A few miles further on Karl, Rab and Beks joined them from the Rabeel and even further along as the escarpment came to near its southern end, they were joined by Barry and Sam from the Mizuki.

Descending down to the plain, this very first ever 'band of brothers', started out south before they would have to turn west and enter the forest which would lead them to the sea. The summer sun was warm with fleeting clouds and a cool breeze making their journey enjoyable, the boys were wearing their summer leggings and smocks. Furs were usually only used as extra covering in winter or at night. There spirits were at an all-time high. This was their first great adventure. High jinks and some verbal ribbing were the order of the day.

Junior, much to the other boys' amusement, came under pressure, when his so-called friend, Jim, let it be known that Junior had the hots for Sasha and could be seen hanging around her at every opportunity.

"He is too scared to talk to her," said Jim.

Junior, embarrassed vehemently, denied any interest in Sasha and what followed was a wrestling match, which to everyone's amusement ended up in a nearby stream.

By this time, it was late afternoon and time to camp for the night. The low hills indicating when it would be time to turn west couldn't be reached before dark, the stream supported a few trees and with dried grasses, wood and dried animal dung, the boys soon had a fire going.

Everyone was tired but it seemed prudent to mount a guard, it wasn't strictly necessary but it seem the right grownup thing to do, two boys stayed up but, without the wherefore all to tell time, when they got fed up, they woke up another two and rolled themselves in their furs and fell almost instantly asleep.

The boys slept in the open under a wonderful display of moon and stars, Junior, however, did not sleep and more familiar with the moon than most, watched its progress through the heavens.

The stars appeared bright and fixed, and as he watched the night sky and wondered just what these points of light were, one very bright star appeared to be moving. It was Venus and he tracked its progress through the night sky. Earlier as he watched, he saw a group of stars directly above the silhouette of the solitary tree and yet when he looked again, the stars had moved. He was not the first of his clan to notice that some stars moved in the night sky most slowly but one or two moved their position in the sky quite significantly and Junior felt, like his father before him, watching the sky was important and he stored these memories away for another day.

The next morning, after some dried meat and water from the stream, the gang set out again, there would be another day and a night before they reached the forest-covered hills where they would then turn west through the forest and descend down to sea level.

The weather continued to be kind and a day's march to fit, young boys was no hardship.

By midday on their third day, they reached the forest to their west, the boys eager to get to their destination ate as they walked, turning left to the west, the gang entered the forest climbing uphill before descending down to the great sea. They came out of the trees on to a sandy beach in a wide bay surrounded on both sides by cliffs. It was late afternoon but the sun was still shining, the boys had a dip in the sea and a bite to eat, and then went exploring and came across a stream running out of the trees into the sea, an ideal spot to set up camp. Firewood and grasses were piled by the stream in preparation for evening. Further exploration was the order of the day, they crossed the stream and headed north for the far end of the bay where the cliffs ran down to the water. There, in large tidal rock pools, were crabs and trapped fish, some big enough to eat, and so with much splashing and lifting of rocks and peering in crevices, a large welcome addition was made to the evening meal. By the time they got back to camp, it was nearly dark.

With a fire lit and food cooked and eaten under the bright stars, the fire gave enough light for the boys to sit around and swap stories, each story becoming funnier and more unbelievable than the last, and one by one, they rolled themselves in their furs and fell asleep.

* * * *

The next morning, Barny suggested that they dam the stream, good fun, but first, a trek to the cliffs at the southern end of the bay. They looked high, maybe there could be caves to explore.

The distance to the end of the beach was about two miles. What started out as a walk on sand and in and out of the water, accompanied by much splashing, soon became a full out race, with fifteen boys naked as the day they were born, racing across the sand whooping and shouting as only the young can do.

There were caves to explore but with no dry access at high tide.

Undaunted, the boys splashed their way in and, with light coming in from a hole in the roof, started to climb higher.

The climb was made easier by what appeared to be roughly cut steps in the rock on the left wall and at about four times higher than a man, a ledge wide enough to walk on, led to the back of the cave and to a horizontal passage on their left, and it was obvious that the ledge had been enlarged. The strike marks made by flint axes were plain to see.

The boys entered the passage which slopped upwards and wasn't completely dark. A faint light ahead made movement easier. With the total lack of fear and the supreme confidence of youth, the boys in single file made their way up the passage.

At the end, they filed out into a large circular chamber, the chamber was about five tens of paces round. Light was supplied by three holes close together in the centre of the chamber, the roof was about the height of five or six men above them and water dripping through the holes fell into an open pit around which someone had built a low stonewall. Nat threw a stone into the pit and after a few seconds, the boys heard the splash as the stone hit water.

It was obvious that the chamber had not been used in a long time, dust and rubble lay all over the floor. The most spectacular features were on the walls, they were drawings of men and animals, the men with spears seemed to be hunting bison, aurochs, delicate antelope and deer, large and small. Benny reckoned that a drawing of a large standing creature was a bear, his dad had told him that in the clan's memory, they used to come down to the river when the fish were running and that they were very dangerous. None had been seen for generations, they had been hunted and trapped and had all been killed or had moved on. Duke reckoned that a large four-legged animal was a mammoth which now only existed in clan's memory and stories. Another wall had drawings of the phases of the moon and drawings that obviously were that of the sun. There were groups of short vertical lines, some with a horizontal line running through them, there were more of these mysterious lines, far too many to count. Junior wondered who had carved on the walls and where were they now, he thought the lines were important and resolved to tell his dad as soon as they got back and with that terrific memory of early man, Junior memorised as much of the details on the wall as he could.

Sam, wandering around the chamber, found another passage leading this time slightly downwards. The boys trooped down until they reached a vertical wall in front of them. At first, this passage appeared to be a dead end until on their left a small passage with steps cut into it, was revealed. Bending double, they followed it down just a few paces until it opened up in to a huge cave, many tens of paces around with a rubble strewn ramp leading up to a huge entrance. Hanging from the roof were bats, far too many to be counted. The smell was overpowering, their droppings covered the cave floor, which seemed to be continuously moving. Junior guessed it was insects feeding on the droppings.

They were standing on a ridge or shelf about the height of four men above the cave floor. The shelf stretched out at least ten spaces on their left and right. There was no obvious way down to the cave floor which Sam observed, "No way, although who would want to go anyway."

Having seen enough, everyone headed back to their camp, only Junior thought about their find.

"No one has lived here for years," Terry said. "No one ever lived here, I mean stayed all the time."

"You're right, of course," Brian said. "That place was a meeting place, and their leaders like Mike, Starr, Murf and Ash stood where we stood and spoke to their clans."

Junior agreed with everyone but something said to him there was more in Junior's life as with everyone in the clans, the concept of a God or indeed Gods had never been entertained. In analysis, life was too difficult and too short to contemplate greater beings.

The boys made their way back to their camp; it was midday when they got there, time for a bite of jerky and the last of the crab. Unfortunately, there were no roots or berries to make a change, a quick dip in the sea and it was time to dam the stream. They went at it with a will using stones, mud, driftwood and seaweed. It soon became a battle between the stream and the gang. With a continuous fight to keep the water in and fixing breeches, the dam got higher and ever wider as the water tried to reach the sea and soon, a respectable pond was born, and boys being boys, a mud fight was next, sand scooped up from their own private pool was used to pelt the nearest neighbour. It was immaterial from which clan the target belonged truly. This band of friends had become a band of brothers and before they knew it, the sun was going down on what turned out to be their last hurrah as children.

Chapter Nine
Attack on the Mizuki

The next morning shortly after dawn, the boys set out to return home, a final dip and they moved away from the beach, into the trees. The gradient increasing as they headed for the great plain, and before midday, they reached the edge of the trees and looked out on to the great plain. Leaving the shelter of the trees, they noticed a line of people heading south. The boys were about to shout, and go out and find out what this trek was all about but something in the demeanour of the line of people, which they now noticed included children, stopped them.

One of the people in the line, a woman carrying a baby, fell and didn't immediately get up. Men came from the rear of the line and started to beat the woman with sticks while she lay on the ground, and with some shouting, which even the boys could hear, made others in the line help the woman up and support her. It now became apparent that some of the people in the line were tied together. Slowly, the column moved off.

A terrible foreboding fell on the boys. Where did these apparent prisoners come from. As one, they raced off heading for the home caves of the nearest clan, the Mizuki. It had taken the gang two days to get to the trees, but such was their desperation to go home, they reached the Mizuki just as it was getting dark. The miles were no distance at all to boys, desperate to find if their families were safe and well.

When they arrived at the home caves, a scene of blood and horror made worse by the dark awaited them. There were mutilated bodies everywhere; mostly men and boys with just a few women. Some of the bodies were unrecognisable, their skulls caved in with terrible force. The ground outside the caves was dark with blood. Suddenly, Sam let out a scream, knelt and held his dead father in his arms, sobbing uncontrollably. Barry, mad with dread, searched for his father. He found him only recognisable by the missing pinkie of his left hand; the sight of his mutilated father was too much. He collapsed unconscious on top of the body. Terry, Adam and Brian picked him up and carried him away from that terrible scene.

Junior took charge, "We can't stay here, although it's dark, we must move on to the Rabeel caves."

Barry and Sam were in no fit to travel, the rest of the gang supported and half carried them on the dark journey to the Rabeel caves. They arrived just after dawn and were relieved to find everything was normal.

Rabeel boys, Karl, Rab and Beks along with Sam and Barry, stayed to tell their clan the terrible story. Everyone else took to their heel for their home caves, more miles along the escarpment; they arrived at the home of the Bureen, stopping only to catch their breath. They left their clansmen, Terry, Adam and Brian to explain. Miles further on the next stop, the Moree, leaving Barny, Nat and Duke to explain to their clan. The Moyan boys ran on to their home caves, arriving totally exhausted and unable to speak coherently, they just lay down on the ground to recover.

Anything out of the ordinary always attracted attention. A crowd gathered round and waited for the boys to recover. Mike and Fred appeared, and when sufficiently recovered, Junior told their story.

The clan could hardly credit what they were hearing. Mike immediately made plans to mount an expedition to the Mizuki home caves, it was late in the day but the Moree clan were not too far away so Mike ordered the hunters to set out for their nearest neighbours, travelling at night was difficult but it was an emergency.

Further plans entailed, at first light, the followers' team would leave, followed by as many men and woman as possible carrying as much supplies as possible.

* * * *

Earlier, the Moyan hunters arrived at the home caves of the Moree to find only the old and the very young. Everyone else was heading for the Mizuki home. The Moyan hunters decided to rest up until dawn and making best speed should make it to the Mizukis by mid-afternoon.

On arriving at the other clans' caves, it was the same story; nearly everyone had left for the Mizuki caves.

* * * *

The following morning, the rest of the Moyan set off. As they walked, Fred quizzed Mike on his plans, "We must rescue the Mizuki survivors. By the boys' account, the captives and the monsters who did it are making slow progress across the plain, they've had a good head start but our hunters are determined and will be travelling light."

"And then?" said Fred

"We charge and free the Mizuki survivors."

"And then?"

"What?" said Mike.

Fred said, "We can't allow these monsters to live. If they can get back to where they came from, more might come."

Mike was silent for a moment as the implications sank in.

"Then we must kill them all," he said. In the long history of memories of the clans, no man had deliberately taken the life of another.

By the time the tribes met up at the scene of the Mizuki massacre, the horrific scene made every one almost mad with anger so strong that some were literally shaking and howling. Never in the memory of the five clans anything like this had ever happened.

Willy and a few of the hunters had already moved out to scout ahead but it took all the authority of the clan leaders to stop everyone charging off in pursuit of the monsters and their prisoners. The four clan chiefs met; plans made.

Even although it was late in the afternoon, the remaining hunters lead by Terry of the Bureen were sent out to link up with Willy and his men, the main body of the clan, set out behind them.

Earlier, Willy and five hunters had left the scene of carnage with a determination to wreak revenge on these human monsters. They travelled light, carrying neither food nor water, only their hunting spears. Experienced as they were, they had no difficulty following the trail from the Mizuki home caves and although a long way behind, were catching up fast. Some miles further on and just before dark, they came across the body of a woman and an infant. By the state of the woman's wraps, it appeared that she had been murdered and raped, probably after death.

It is impossible to describe the fury of these peaceable men, their bodies were consumed by shaking and shrieking, and it was some time before Willy was able to pull them away from the scene. They ran on until dark then lay down and slept fitfully.

The following morning, the main body of the four clans and the survivors of the Mizuki clan, the boys, Barry and Sam, moved out on to the plain now following a well sign-posted trail.

Having left earlier, Terry and the rest of the hunters continued to follow Willy and his men, and soon found the sad scene of the murdered woman and her infant, again their rage knew no bounds.

Willy and his men continued their forced march. It started to rain and while they kept on the move, it wasn't so bad but, just before dark, they sighted the slow-moving column, and were forced to stop and wait for the rest of the clan. What followed was a most miserable cold night with no shelter or coverings.

There were now three bodies of the clans on the move. Willy and five hunters now shadowing at a distance the human monsters and their prisoners, behind them, Terry and the rest of the hunters rapidly catching up and behind them all the able-bodied of the four remaining clans. Mid-afternoon, Terry and the remaining hunters, nineteen in all, caught up with Willy, and continued to shadow and by dusk, the rest of the clans were in sight. Willy sent a runner back to tell them to keep coming despite the dark, before midnight, all the clans were together and plans made.

The human monsters appeared to number about ten and another ten, their prisoners less than ten and ten, and another ten including children and babies. The clan hunters numbered ten, ten and four, and too many other clansmen to count both men and women, and Barry and

Sam, the Mizuki boys. There were only two things on everyone's mind, rescue and revenge.

The leaders; Mike, Ash, Murf and Star, debated and came up with a plan.

Willy and ten hunters under cover of the night were to circle and get ahead of the human monsters. As dawn broke, they were to shout and scream taking attention away from the main attack. At the last moment, Mike ordered Barry and Sam to join them. Mike felt that this would be the safest place for them. Willy and his men and the boys moved out in a wide circle to get in front of their enemy.

Quietly, Willy said to his men, "You five, move to my right; ten paces apart." To the other five, "Move to my left ten paces. I want you all to lie down and wait until dawn when it is light enough for me to see you all. I will stand up as it gets light. I want you to keep looking for me. When I stand up, this is the signal for you all to stand and shout and yell."

Shortly after dawn, Willy and his hunters and the boys started as planned, shouting and screaming, the human monsters with their attention to the south didn't notice the main attack until it was too late, the battle was short and bloody, for the first time ever, the people of the clans killed fellow humans.

When the attack started, two of the enemy turned and ran south towards Willy and his men. One brute ran straight at Willy and received a spear in his belly, his momentum kept him going, and with Willy's spear wrenched from his hands and the base stuck on the ground, the man was lifted off of his feet and would have performed a perfect arc had the spear not broken on the downward arc. He was dead before he hit the ground.

The other man ran straight at Barry and Sam knocking them both over. Sam was on his feet in an instant, ran after him, dived on to his legs and caught one and held on grimly. The man turned, raised his club to smash Sam's head but the blow never came. Barry jumped in the air to gain height and smashed his club on the monster's head. He went down. Barry hit him again and again and again and again, and would have continued except Willy grabbed the boy in a bear hug and gradually calmed him down.

In a matter of a few minutes, all the human monsters were dead, a silence descended over the scene, broken only by the crying of children and some people being sick.

There was nothing else to do but make the slow sad journey back to their homes. There was no joy at the rescue of the Mizuki survivors. The human monsters left where they had fallen. The clan's leaders dispatched a group of men and women to the Mizuki home caves to clean up and lay out the bodies for burial. At the same time, the human monsters were searched and for the first time, the clan discovered metal.

Death among the clans was common, and always a sad occasion and burial was important mainly for reasons of hygiene and the prevention of loved ones' remains disturbed by animals. Burial had no religious significance at this time, but with so many bodies to bury, all the four clans and the survivors of the Mizuki gathered to prepare the burial site and lay the dead in a mass grave. Someone threw a few flowers, a distraught woman threw her husband's fur coverings quickly followed by other belongings of the dead Mizuki. The widow of Merz, the flint knapper threw his precious tools into the grave, the widow of Jebb, the medicine man threw in his bags of herbs and potions and the Mizuki clan were no more.

People started talking, asking why. How could humans from another place do what they did to us? What made them do it? In all of the history of the clans, nothing like this had ever happened? And gradually, a dawning, could it happen again?

After the burials, the people were reluctant to go their separate ways. Star, the leader of the next nearest clan, the Rabeel suggested that everyone adjourn to the Rabeel home caves to this end. He ordered his women to leave immediately and prepare food for all.

Of the Mizuki, seventeen woman and eight children survived in addition to Barry and Sam. The clan leaders debated about splitting the survivors to the remaining four clans.

In practical terms, this would be the best plan making the remaining clans that bit stronger. The problem was the survivors were in shock and didn't want to be separated nor did they want to stay in their home caves. A compromise was reached, the Moree would take them all in and it was hoped that through time, some would move to other clans.

Shortly after that terrible day and the demise of the Mizuki, the four remaining clans' Chiefs met to discuss the implications.

Mike started the discussion, "I believe it's too late in the season for another attack, but I think they will be back next summer."

Ash agreed and said, "We need to send out men to try and find out where they come from."

Star of the Rabeel made a good point, "Can we afford to lose men on such an expedition, they will have to be hunters and we need all the hunters we have."

After much signing and talk, they agreed that an expedition of eight hunters, two from each clan, would leave on a spying expedition in early spring. They also agreed to pool all of their resources and on that day, another step was taken towards nationhood.

Part Three

Chapter Ten
The Vornay clan – The Horse People

When the clans looked out in the morning, the east beyond their range of vision was a range of mountains. Beyond these mountains lived more humans. They were the Vornay, horse people. Long ago, they captured, broke and trained the wild ponies of the plains, and along with early breeds of sheep and goats, provided most of their needs. They were as one with their animals, wandering the plain always looking for fresh pastures, which were becoming harder to find.

The weather pattern was slowly changing, becoming dryer with the mountains to their west stopping much of the rain.

The people lived in extended family groups and were in loose contact with each other, they had known for some time that they would have to move.

Things came to a head in July. The Fox family disappeared. Their animals found wandering near their last camp. There was found the body of Fox, the family head and his two sons and his brother. Like the clans, the Vornay were in shock and rage, and immediately, horsemen rode out to inform all the families. When they were all gathered, riders set out south following the slow painful trail of the surviving Fox family and their captors.

Like the clans, they quickly found the raiders and their captives. There could be only one outcome when angry men on horseback attacked men on foot, even if the horsemen had no fighting experience. Once again, there were no survivors to flee south to report to Rufus.

After the shock and grief of the families, John the leader of the biggest and therefore, the senior family gathered all the families.

He was getting old and feeling his age not yet thirty. He was almost bald and what hair he had was grey, more importantly for him, he had broken a leg when trapped under a fallen horse. The leg had healed but it was twisted and he walked with a limp, and now years later, he was in constant pain, his enthusiasm for change was long gone but as the leader, he felt responsible for everyone's well-being.

He stood and said what everyone was thinking, "We need to move on to a new place, we have lived on these plains for as long as anyone can remember but the rains have been getting less year after year, and now we have lost our Fox family to evil people from the south. Now is the time to move. Where should we go? This is the question I am asking."

Buster stood and spoke, "If we move, it can't be south. We know what lies to the east. It's just plain, I believe, we must try and find a way through the western mountains."

And so, after much talk and preparation, a party of six Vornay, their ponies and extra baggage mounts left to cross the mountains in search of a possible safer land or maybe allies.

Buster, the leader of these explorers, was accompanied by his wife, Lilly; their son, Jude; and Alice, their daughter; his brother, Blake and his wife, Poppy and five baggage ponies, distributing their livestock to other families. They carried all they owned in the world with them.

On approach to the western mountains, the view was daunting, first impressions were that passage was impossible, men could climb but horses couldn't. Blake suggested, "We ride south to find a safe passage."

Buster said, "Best to move north. We don't want to meet more of those southern savages."

It was agreed and the Vornay explorers turned north following the base of the mountain range day after day. After ten days and one day with no prospect of a way through the range, Buster was beginning to think south might have been a better bet, and as they camped for the night said as much, "One more day and if we can't find a way over the mountains, we will turn south."

Blake disagreed, "We have come too far north to turn back now, this range can't go on forever, there must be a way through."

Two days later, they reached a river but instead of it running east away from the mountains, it ran west straight towards the mountain range.

"There must be a way through," said Buster. "Where else can the water go?"

They followed the river west for half a day, and into a narrow canyon with towering cliffs on each side, the constriction of the canyon caused the river to run fast and turbulent and didn't bode well for a safe passage. However, the July dry weather meant the water level was low. And the party splashed on in the shallows, they reached a bend with the river flowing left and north and rounding it the canyon widened the water slowed, and on their right-hand side of the river, a flat flood plain a hundred paces wide and hundreds of paces long. It was ideal for an overnight camp, allowing the horses to wander free.

The band had been travelling for over a month, stopping and collecting berries, tubers and occasionally running down a deer or whatever they came across, but everyone was getting tired and stale. This idyllic pasture was perfect for a few days' rest especially for the horses. When Buster suggested it, there were no objectors. There were even a few scraggy trees growing out of cracks in the lower part of the cliff face and plenty of firewood deposited by the river on the flood plain, camp was set up, poles and hides removed from the baggage horses and their tents erected. Buster and Blake started to prepare a fire, the method they used was the bow drill. While Buster started to rotate the drill with the bow, the end of the drill grinding away in the hollow of the fire board created combustible dust, which with the friction, soon became a glowing coal which was transferred to a piece of tree bark held by Blake. He added dry grasses, ground up dried horsehair and blowing gently, soon had a flame going which he transferred to the bed of twigs prepared by his brother. Lilly prepared their wooden boles, unpacked the stones that when heated, provided the hot water for cooking.

The Vornay were not good fishermen but they didn't need to be on this bountiful planet, the empty panniers from the pack horses made excellent baskets. Alice and Poppy stood in the river and the fish just seemed to swim into the baskets. Meanwhile, Jude went exploring, following the river to the end of the flood plain and once again, the cliffs closed in, Jude waded out to a sandbar ten of ten paces away and was relieved to find the water was not too deep. At the western end of the sandbar, Jude saw another sandbar, this time as he waded towards it, the water became too deep for him and as a non-swimmer, he turned back to the first sandbar.

Jude considered going back to collect his pony and either riding him or holding on to his neck. He knew he would be able to reach the second sandbar but he knew his father would not let him go on alone and at thirteen summers, he was and felt he was a man. The only alternative of reaching the second sandbar was wading to the cliff and looking for a route west along the cliff. It seemed possible, a ledge partway along looked promising so he started climbing using fingers and toes, he inched his way up and along towards the ledge. He was inches away when his left handhold gave way and he fell screaming thirty feet towards the river and worse, on the way down, he struck the cliff face and fell unconscious into the water.

On the floodplain, everyone heard Jude's cry and raced to the river's edge, and on to the first sandbar from there, Jude could be seen lying face down in the water near the second sandbar. They all waded out to the rescue but the water was too deep. Only Alice was able to swim out to her brother but she wasn't the first to reach him. Max, Jude's pony, was way ahead of Alice and when she reached Jude, Max was nuzzling him with no effect.

The water was too deep to stand. Alice grabbed Max's mane with her left hand and in her right grabbed her brother's left hand. The horse needed little encouragement, and swam and scrambled on to the sandbar, when Alice found her feet, she dragged Jude half out of the water and still face down, she collapsed on to the sand.

The rest of the horses had congregated on the western edge of the flood plain and when the humans whistled on them, they plunged into the water all of them even the packhorses and headed for the first sandbar and when united with their human halves, everyone mounted and plunged into the deeper water towards the second sandbar.

Alice was recovering but Jude was still unconscious. Buster and Blake lifted him onto Max crossways with his head hanging down on the horse's flanks. This caused him to cough and bring up some water. Buster and Blake held his legs and pushed Jude until he was almost vertically upside down while his mother, Lilly, started smacking him hard on his back. The result of this instinctive unpractised first aid was Jude vomited more water, and started lapsing in and out of consciousness.

Buster said to Poppy, "You're the lightest, mount his horse and hold him upright, we'll support you." With Jude held tightly by Poppy and jammed between Buster and Blake's horses with both men holding on to Max's mane, the party slowly set off back to the flood plain.

Jude stripped, dried, wrapped in furs and laid down near the fire. That's all the Vornay could do. No one prayed, they didn't have any gods to pray to.

Someone stayed up with Jude all night as he gradually surfaced back to conscious. By the morning, he was awake and feeling sorry for himself and covered with bruises.

When Buster found out from his son what had actually happened, he walked away in anger at his foolhardy climb and it would have been very hard on him if Lilly had not interceded. She drew herself to her full height of nearly five feet one, "Don't you dare, the boy has been through enough without you making things worse."

And like all good husbands everywhere, Buster knew when to bow down and said, "Yes, dear."

While Jude recuperated, Buster and Blake decided to take their horses and scout beyond the second sandbar. To turn back now was unthinkable and so the next morning, with encouragement from their wives, only too glad to get rid of them so they could attend to their patient, the two brothers set out to follow the river west to the first sandbar and then riding their horses over the deep part to the second sandbar. At the western end of the bar, a mere hundred paces away, the river spread out and appeared shallow with rocks jutting out of the water. The men and horses slowly picked their way over the shallows keeping to the right side and after a few hundred paces of slow progress, the river again turned left and north, but in front of them on their right, was another flood plain just a few feet above the level of the water. The horses scrambled up onto the plain and were able to trot for at least a mile with the only obstacles being the debris of logs and trees left by the river when in flood. At the end of the floodplain, the ground slopped down gently to the great plain they were through and on to the great western plain.

They decided to go no further and headed back to camp. On the way, Buster saw several caves set in to the cliff and noted them for future use.

Chapter Eleven
The Great Plain

Three days later, the Vornay expedition moved out on to the great plain and immediately saw that this plain was more fertile than their previous home, fed by the retreating glacier and a higher rainfall. Animal life was far more plentiful. This plain abounded with bison, auroch, deer, even horses and herd animals they failed to identify.

Jude was much better, and made light of his bruises and stiffness.

On their first night on the plain, a council of war was held with only one subject on the agenda, where next. Buster advocated to continue west. Blake said, "Let's go back and fetch all the families, this plain is ideal for us and our animals."

"Yes, but what if this is the home turf of the people who attacked us!" And so, it was agreed to press on west.

Their journey across the great plain began, it was obvious that animal life in this part of the world was far more numerous. The herds of horse were cautious but seemed unafraid and appeared interested in their fellow horses with the funny looking appendages on their backs.

Blake commented, "I don't believe they have never seen humans before or as Buster said, perhaps they have never been hunted before. This bodes well for us, this plain might not have any people on it."

With the benefit hunting on horseback and the more fertile plain, no one went hungry. It was becoming obvious that this great plain was far better than the lands east of the mountains, Poppy echoed all their thoughts, "You know, if all of our people moved to this side of the mountains, life will be better."

"Provided," said her husband, "that those murderers from the south don't live here as well."

Day followed day after day with no end in sight, the summer weather in June had been fine with almost cloudless skies and the nights not too cold, no one could remember when it last rained. At night, usually in the shelter of a rocky tor, talk was of the future.

"We can't go on like this forever," sighed Poppy

"I agree but we can't go back now," said Buster. "But I noticed as we made camp tonight to the south and west there was a layer of clouds on the horizon, I think the clouds were above hills, if I am right, this endless plain may end there."

The next morning, the Vornay's ever-westward journey veered a few degrees south.

Two days later, a row of hills appeared on the horizon and as Buster said, "This journey should go no further."

It was agreed and if there was nothing to report about the hills. They would turn around and search for a suitable place to use as a permanent camp. After which, Blake and Poppy would head east through the mountains and meet with the rest of the Vornay, and hopefully, persuade the whole clan to move west to the more fertile and abundant great plain especially with its herds of wild horses.

Jude asked if he could go back with his uncle and aunt.

Buster laughed and said, "You just want to show off to your friends and tell tall stories of our journey and your heroism." Jude, mortified by his father's put down, knew in his heart that his dad wasn't wrong.

Lilly, like all mothers, didn't want to see her wee boy go and said as much that she was dead against this return journey through the mountains, "It nearly killed you once, what do you want, another chance for the mountain to kill you."

Buster intervened, "He's no longer a boy. He will soon be looking for a wife. Maybe that's the reason he wants to go back."

Blake listened with an amusement at this exchange and said to Lilly, "Let the poor boy go, Poppy and I will look after him, it's time to give him his head."

On the afternoon of the third day, the horse people approached a large tor set on a hill well above the plain, an obvious destination for a midday break.

Chapter Twelve
A Meeting

The clan's summer festival was about to start and everyone was down on the plain preparing. The rough shelters of a few years ago, thanks to the discovery of the needle, had improved in leaps and bounds. No longer was a shelter tied to the size of a couple of animal skins, several skins sewn together with overlapping closely sewn waterproof seems led to a plethora of shapes and sizes.

Hunters moved out for one last hunt before the festivities.

In the aftermath of the slaughter of the Mizuki, the clan hunters often worked together to hunt. And on this day, eleven hunters led by Willy were moving east and north in search of a suitable herd to attack, a large tor set on top of a hill would make a good observation point, climbing on top of the largest rock would allow a hunter to see for miles.

Unaware of each other, the two parties headed for the same tor.

Willy and the hunters rounded the east side of the tor while simultaneously the Vornay rounded the west side. They almost missed each other. Felix a hunter spotted the packhorses and let out a shout of amazement.

The Vornay reigned and turned around, and came face to face with the clan, everything stopped. The clan could hardly believe their eyes, here were five humans sitting on top of wild horses with a line of horses behind obviously carrying all their possessions. Were these the murderers of the Mizuki clan?

In their turn, the horse people looked down in wonder at the hunters unlike themselves. They were not bare legged, dressed in skins and furs with suitable holes cut in them as required. They wore no fur capes tied round their necks instead each man had leggings bound with leather chord and a coat or smock not with holes for arms but material enclosed around their arms and attached to the coat, the material of their clothes appeared to be leather but treated in such a way that it appeared soft and pliable. Each man had a leather bag around his shoulders held with straps and carried a wooden spear taller than himself, and almost unbelievably, the men were almost bare faced not like the Vornay with their months of facial hair, only Jude was young enough to be beardless. Were these the attackers from the south?

The two groups looked at each other and froze. Time slowed; Willy stared at Alice. He had never seen a more beautiful girl, tall for a female. She was nearly as tall as him, obviously slim under her furs. She had blonde hair and blue eyes. Willy had never thought much about beauty until he gazed on her face, he was enchanted.

Alice stared at Willy, slim and unhindered by bulky furs, lightly clad for the summer heat, muscular with no strangely beard and short jet-black hair. He was the most handsome man she had ever seen and she too was enchanted. She smiled. Willy smiled back.

Then it happened, loudly, a horse broke wind. Willy and Alice smiled, then the horse did it again even more loudly, and everyone started to laugh. The impasse was broken and on that day, the world became a better place all because a horse farted.

With the tension broken, the Vornay dismounted and came forward, the hunters at Willy's lead stuck their spears into the ground and walked forward to meet new friends. This first meeting was stilted and awkward. The raising of hands, palms outward, the international sign of peace was all very well but what next. Both languages had nothing in common but with much touching of chests and repeating of names, progress was made.

Alice took it a step further, she took Willy's hand and led him to her horse Theo, and said his name at the touch of her hand. Willy felt weak at his knees, his heart pounded, tentatively, he stroked Theo's neck. Next, Alice leaped on to his back and beckoned Willy to jump on behind her. Willy hummed hawed, and much to the amusement of everyone, tried to climb head and body first. Next, he tried leaping on to Theo's back a la Alice style only to overdo the leap and landed in a heap on the other side of the horse. His audience roared; Willy was mortified. Buster came to his aid and with cupped hands, he was hoisted on to the horse's back. Once mounted and with his arms around the waist of the most beautiful girl in the world, he was in heaven. She urged Theo forward, at first a walk then a trot and finally, a cantor. Willy's terror increased with speed but with his arms around Alice, his terror lessened and changed to enjoyment. He wished this ride would never end.

With Alice and Willy leading, they all headed back towards the clan's summer festival. As the camp came into sight, Willy anticipating problems signed to Alice with a circular motion of his arm indicated that Alice should sit behind him. Not sure quite why, she nevertheless leaped off Theo and leapt on behind him, and with her arms around the most handsome boy in the world, she wished this ride would never end.

When the people saw the approaching column, panic spread. Willy and Alice on Theo were at first too far away to be seen as separate riders on a horse especially as no one had ever seen a man on a horse before, they were unable to interpret what their eyes were seeing.

As these newcomers approached, the men of the clans formed a defence line facing an oncoming enemy, behind them the woman backed up their men folk and behind them the children.

However, as Willy and Alice got closer and eyes were able to focus, the sight of Willy, the bravest hunter astride an animal brought a shout of joy and relief. The clan preparing to defend had stood stiff and erect but at the sight of Willy, everyone relaxed and to Willy's eye, everyone became a wee bit smaller.

Theo approached the line of men, Alice halted him and Willy managed to spring off without making a fool of himself. He beckoned the Vornay and the rest of the hunters to come forward, "We've made friends with these people, we can learn from them and we have much to teach them."

Mike came forward and as Buster dismounted, both men saw in each other that they were the leaders. "Welcome to our festival." Willy intervened and explained to Mike that the horse people didn't speak the language of the clan. What followed again was much touching of chests and saying of names and pointing to objects, meanwhile, the children having seen Willy on one of the beasts knew no fear and crowded round them and with some help from the Vornay, many were lifted up to pat necks and even sit on their backs. The horses bred in captivity, stood patiently while they were stroked and prodded.

Mike and Willy conducted the Vornay around the festival campsite, they were amazed by the size of the tents (thanks to the humble needle). The tent of Ash and Jean, leaders of tent technology, had the fire going inside and food cooking.

Previous festivals, the enlightenment of clans continued. During the summer, they discarded the traditional fur wraps, and now dressed in loose fitting leather, stitched smocks and trousers, skirts, and a new summer fad had arisen. They started to shorten head hair and beards with burning glowing faggots of pine sticks drawn from the fire in the skilled hands of a wife or buddy. Unruly lice infested locks and beards could be shorn quite close to the skin. Emily, wife of Murf of the Bureen, found that a wash of certain common herbs combined with shorter hair killed lice and their eggs.

These conditions cemented the two people. The clans were excited by the possibility and benefits of horses in their hunting, and the Vornay were only too ready to accept the new technology of the needle and who would not want to get rid of hair and body lice, and with that superior memory of our ancient forbears, communications and language came on leaps and bounds. The Vornay learned the language of the clans who in turn absorbed new words from the horse people.

The summer wore on, the Vornay took to the dress of the clans and were gifted suitable living accommodation and in return, started to pass on their skills as horse people. Jude, now fully recovered from his ordeal in the mountain pass, took charge of hunting the wild horses of the plains, once corralled. Herd leaders were slaughtered for meat, as were some stallions. Younger stallions and mares and their young were mixed with the Vornay horses, and the breaking of the wild horses began. The two Mizuki boys, Barry and Sam, proved to be fast learners.

This summer on the plains was the best in living memory. The weather was exceptionally kind, winds were warm and fresh high enough, and combined with the smoke of many fires, the flying biting insects were kept to a minimum. It seemed only to rain at night. New friends made; new skills learned. Everyone felt physically better and healthier.

* * * *

Everyone knew that Willy and Alice were destined to be together. Mike and Buster agreed to give them a tent of their own, pitched some way from the centre of things, which was a good thing as the more sexually experienced Willy took Alice on a path of joy and ecstasy that sometimes could be heard all over the camp.

Alice was always pretty but now she just blossomed and Willy seemed to stand taller.

Chapter Thirteen
Caves Abandoned

Hunting continued.

The five packhorses now donated to the clans, and with increasing riding experience, hunting was transformed. Injuries much reduced, hunts were concluded earlier, and kills could be dragged back for dissection with less effort.

The capture and breaking of wild horses became the second priority after the hunt.

The summer wore on, the unspoken thought of nearly everyone was that wintering in the cold, wet, dripping caves on the escarpment to say the least was not appealing.

Murf and heavily pregnant Emily came up with an alternative. There were many flat areas on the escarpment especially below the old Mizuki caves but still within the tree line and not too far from the great plain, the trees offered some protection from the winter storms.

Murf put forward his plans, "We can move or build new tents on the flat area, and the trees will help protect us."

Yan, the Moyan medicine man said, "But we always have lived in our caves."

"Yes," Murf replied, "but can you keep a cave warm, can you stop water dripping down on us, can you stop draughts keeping us cold all winter long?"

"Yes, we can we build walls to stop the draughts."

"But do they work?" Yan was silent.

On a warm late summer evening for the first time ever, a meeting held, everyone, young, old, children, Vornay and a few interested Vornay horses met round a central fire. The atmosphere was electric, children ran wild shushed by adults, no one knew why they were there but it all seemed good fun and important. Some of the woman started to sing about a young man who kept falling of a horse. No names mentioned but Terry, the hunter from the Bureen, suddenly under his short beard had a very red face.

Willy and Alice sat side by side, Willy's arm around Alice's waist. They had seldom been apart since they met. Buster and Lilly had never seen their daughter so happy.

Mike stood up, as did the leaders of the other clans. Ash, Murf and Star, he raised his arms for quiet.

"I, no, I mean we," indicating Ash, Murf and Star, "have been talking together and talking to some of you, and I am asking you now before the summer ends, do you want to go back to our caves?"

There were murmurs from everyone. After this glorious summer on the plain, no one wanted to go back to a wet dank cave.

"Murf has a plan," Star said. "We all move our tents up to the large flat area below the old Mizuki caves, the trees will help protect us from the worst of winter. Most of you now have fires in your tents, hunting with horses has been the best thing that has happened to us. We have never been more successful. We can add extra hides to our tents to help keep out the cold and who knows next year or the next, we could build a wall to the north to give us more protection, there is easy access on to the escarpment for the horses."

In modern parlance, it was a 'no brainer'. No one wanted to go back to the caves and the bonds of nationhood, already embryonic, reinforced even more.

Everyone decided there and then that a start would be made immediately on a winter camp. Murf took charge, the main workforce was the older ex-hunters now almost redundant with the introduction of horses. Although as horses started to become available, some old hunters were just itching to go back to the prestige of the hunter.

Jean organised the women to process skins. Tam, the Moree flint knapper, passed on his latest skills in needle making to the other clan knappers, the demand for needles started to outstrip production, after all, the life of a bone needle was short, animal hide no matter how well processed was tough on the needles. Eventually, boys from all the clans joined the boys from the Moree sifting through mountains of animal carcasses for suitable bones to be smashed into smaller pieces and then prepared for the knappers.

The camp buzzed with activity. Sewn hides transported to the now cleared space on the escarpment and one more change took place in the clans' lives. No longer did women cook for their men, folk and families. The demand for labour was so intense that a communal kitchen was set up to feed everyone, which in turn led to new ways in food production.

Burying meat wrapped in leaves and left in a fire pit of hot coals to cook had always been a favourite. This method continued on an almost industrial scale and nationhood again became that bit closer.

The population of the four clans was almost two-hundred and it says much for early man that things moved on so swiftly but, of course, there was no health and safety. There were no human rights to breach and far more importantly, there was a hierarchy within the clans. Individuals knew their place in the scheme and seldom complained.

Chapter Fourteen
Fred comes down from the Caves

The life of the clans was changing fast in less than a year. The people had met and bonded with a people who were not clan, they had already cast off their smelly hide wraps and almost daily new designs of clothes paraded around the camp (something that still happens to this day). Hair and beards burned shorter, and with herb washes, the scourge of lice and ticks almost eliminated.

With the help of the Vornay and their horses, hunting was more successful and easier. The wet, cold, dark, draughty caves were about to become a thing of the past. Hide tents increased in complexity, sophistication and insulation.

The people didn't know it yet but their health and longevity was increasing in leaps and bounds. The herb washes had extended beyond hair and beards.

What the clans' people did know was, they were happier, better fed than they had ever been.

The problem of the monsters from the south and the clans' intention to send spies south to find the monsters who had wiped out the Mizuki hadn't happened, but when Buster told of the killing of the Fox family, a scouting mission once again became a priority. It was too late in the season for this year but next spring, a scouting mission would head south.

Summer moved on; the weather held but nights were cooler. The great hunt was not far away and Mike turned his thoughts to Fred who had stayed on at the Moyan caves, charting the shadows of the sun. He summoned Junior, "Go home and ask your father, does he know when the plains animals will start their journey south."

Junior now older and bolder said, "Of course, he knows. I will go and fetch him. Can I take my horse?"

Junior took Rory, his horse, up on to the escarpment by the old Mizuki caves stopping for a while to watch the activity as the winter camp took shape, he headed north along the well-worn path to his home cave and his dad.

Fred had been alone for months and talking to clansmen who had come back to the caves to collect belongings. He began to understand that the caves might be abandoned.

He was living on dried meat and water, and had observed the decreasing shadow of the sun. He recorded midsummer and the increasing length of the 'lone pine's' shadow as summer turned towards autumn.

He missed his wife, his son and daughter a good deal. He just wanted to get away and join the world of people but something kept him there. He knew that the site of the lonesome pine was too far away from the clans to be useful and so he woke one morning with the answer. If the clans were not coming back to the caves and the lonesome pine was too far away, he would build a new lonesome pine near the clans. Why didn't he think of this before?

As Fred sat alone outside the home caves cheered by his new plan, an apparition appeared. Junior riding a horse, Fred could not believe his eyes, here was his son towering above him and sitting on an animal.

"Dad, you won't believe what has been happening while you were up here, we met these people, the Vornay. They capture and use horses. Buster, their leader, gave me Rory here. And Mike sent me up to fetch you. He wants to know when to start the autumn hunt."

Junior and his dad headed down the escarpment. Fred refused to join his son on Rory to which Junior was just as glad.

Fred was in fur wraps, and his hair and beard infested. When they arrived, June appeared and dragged him off for hair singes and a herb wash, and Jean of the Moree supplied some proper clothes.

When Fred appeared to talk to Mike, he was uncomfortable but a picture of sartorial elegance.

"Well," said Mike, "when will the herds start to migrate south?"

Fred spoke, "Last year and the year before, the herds started to move south three new moons and ten days and another ten days after midsummer."

"Yes," said Murf, "but what of this summer?"

Fred responded, "I think they will start to migrate in ten days and another ten days, and another two days from today."

Fred's prediction was accurate, the autumn hunt was a success and his reputation made again, and so he asked if he could have a meeting with the four clan leaders. His reputation was such that a meeting was arranged, and Fred told them of his plans for a new site for the lonesome pine. "You don't want to move that old tree here," enquired Murf.

"No, of course not, that would be impossible. No, I want an area clear of trees so they won't shade the sun."

"And in place of the tree?" asked Mike. Fred hesitated that what he wanted was a big ask.

"Off the many tors on the plain, there are lots of stone splinters that have broken off, and are lying on the ground; some taller than a man and just as thick as a man around his chest. We could bring one below to the village, dig a hole and mount it upright. That would be a replacement for the old tree."

Starr said, "Stone that size would be too heavy to move." Fred's idea wasn't popular but Mike appreciated the contribution to the clans made by him and didn't dismiss the idea out of hand instead Fred was to select a suitable site near the village and scout for a suitable stone and then in the spring work might begin.

The autumn hunt topped off the clans' successful year and with the ever-closer integration of the people, no one would starve during the harsh months to come.

Chapter Fifteen
Second Journey to the Sea Cave

Not too far away, Buster was thinking it was time to return to the Vornay before the winter set in, the coming autumn rains might make the journey through the mountains impossible. He assumed rightly that Alice would not want to go without Willy, and as the foremost hunter, Willy couldn't be spared. If the Vornay were to leave the plains beyond the western mountains and move to the more fertile plains of the clan, representatives of the clans had best accompany them on their journey through the mountains.

Buster met with the clan leaders, they all sat down outside the grand tent of the Moree.

"Before winter, we should return to the western plain where we will re-join our people."

Ash said, "Will you be coming back?"

"Coming back!!! Of course, I will tell every one of the fertile western plain and of the people there and their way of life. I will tell them we all should make the journey through the mountains and, if you permit, join you or at least live side by side with you. There is plenty of room and together, we should not be afraid of the monsters from the south."

Mike couldn't think of and didn't want to make any objection, "Some of us should go with you and meet your clan."

So, it was agreed. Alice would stay as would Jude to help with the horse training and hunting and corral building during the coming winter.

Who from the clan should go with Buster and his family to the home of the Vornay?

Barry and Sam were candidates, newly proven with horses and with no family, they readily agreed and looked forward with enthusiasm to the journey, someone older was needed and Jock, the young hunter of the Moyan now with a new wife, Isla of the Rabeel was happy to go on a great adventure.

On a cloudy September day while the clans were gathered together to say goodbye to Buster, Lilly, Blake and Poppy along with Barry, Sam, Jock and Isla, the weather broke torrential rainstorm. Fierce icy winds from the north lashed on to the plain, Buster had left it too late for the return journey through the mountains.

As it turned out, overwintering with the clans was a good thing. The Vornay assisted in hunting and advised on the building and corralling of horses during the bleak winter months.

The winter quarter on the escarpment was becoming a village. Although all the four clans would be living together, the people of one clan wanted to build alongside their own and this led to problems and arguments about position. The prevailing winds were north-west, tents built in the southeast of the village offered the best protection; it was complicated and there would be losers. Junior came up with an idea to help the clan leaders make decisions. He remembered the drawings in the cave by the sea, he searched and found a flat vertical rock face not too far from the village and proceeded to draw an almost scale model of the village and surrounding features, streams, middens, paths and corrals.

When he showed it to the clan leaders, Mike, Ash, Murf and Star spent hours debating and arguing and eventually came up with a plan for the whole village. Some families were not happy when they found that they would be relocated but under the strong leadership of the clan leaders, gradually a cohesive winter village started to take shape.

Fred, in a half-hearted search for his new site, remembered Junior's visit to the sea cave and their mysterious drawings.

The weather had turned cold but the journey was best made before true winter set in.

At dawn on a cold November day, Junior on horseback led his father, unhappily mounted on another horse set out for the sea. On horseback, they took just a day to reach the cave exactly as described by Junior.

It was too late in the day to enter the cave. With the horses hobbled, the two Moyan settled down for a cold night. There was no time to set up a camp, a fire lit and the two settled down for a cold night with only their furs to keep out the cold.

Next morning after a meagre bite, the tide was low enough for the pair to enter the cave without getting their feet too wet. Junior led his father up the rough steps to the back of the cave and left into the passage, at the end of the passage. They entered into the chamber; nothing had changed. Water still dripped from the three holes in the roof and fell into the hole in the floor, the low wall around the hole was unchanged.

The chamber was almost circular and covered with drawings, representations of men, animals, the sun, and the phases of the moon and a whole series of short vertical lines. The drawings of men and animals were obviously hunting scenes possibly to show the best way to hunt a particular animal. One showed a large animal standing on two legs and surrounded by hunters with spears.

Junior said, "I think Benny said he thought that the animal might be a bear, his dad told him about them."

The short vertical lines chiselled into the rock intrigued Fred. At first, they made no sense. He counted the lines; they were grouped in tens. Above them were phases of the moon. Then it was obvious, it was what he was already doing; counting the days in groups of ten between one new moon and the next.

Chiselled into the rock above the moons were drawings, which they interpreted as the sun. These drawings, unlike the moons and the days between the moon, were not in orderly straight lines. The first sun was the highest, each sun was lower than the one on its left until the chiselled suns started to get higher again.

Fred was having difficulty trying to understand what all these moons, suns and the huge number of lines meant. When outside the cave, the sun came out from behind a cloud and above the three holes in the roof allowed a shaft of sunlight to light up the gloom; instantly Fred understood, the highest sun was midsummer. The lowest sun was midwinter. It was possible to count the days between one midsummer and the next and thanks to the mysterious builders of this wall, Fred could now produce a calendar. Was it as easy as that?

Re-examining the ten and two phases of the moon and under them the small chiselled lines grouped in tens, he noticed that not all groups had three and ten marks. Some had three and ten and a one and surprisingly it appeared that a few of the extra ones had been chiselled out. Fred knew why, he already had a problem with the midsummer of one year and the phases of the moon on midsummer day the next year. It appeared that the makers of this wonderful place had had the same problem.

There had to be an answer but today was not that day. Junior was keen to get home. This cave brought back too many bad memories and besides, with some hard riding, they might be able to get there before dark. Fred reluctantly agreed with his son but his buttocks, legs and back disagreed.

The real reason for Junior's hurry to go home was Sasha. He was now old enough to have a mate and now was the time to speak to her and her father and mother. Although he knew they would agree; after all the two of them had been disappearing into the forest all summer. They thought no one noticed but everyone did.

The two riders left the beach, entered the trees and riding uphill, came out onto the plain. The last time Junior had done this, he came out on the plain as a boy but, in a few short days he had become a young man.

When Fred and Junior arrived back at the village, Junior went in search of Sasha and found her with her mother.

"About time," her mother said, "we need to make preparations for the celebration."

"What celebration?" enquired Junior.

"I haven't had a chance to tell him yet," said Sasha. "I am pregnant."

Junior didn't know what to say or do. Although he should not have been surprised, at the age of nearly fourteen, his hormones were rampant.

Ella, Sasha's mother, experienced and ever-practicable, started preparing for Junior to join her household until suitable accommodation was available.

Fred and Jean wanted the couple to move in with them, something Mike agreed with. He knew the value of father and son working together, and so the couple moved into Fred and Jean's hut while Mike quietly expedited a hut for the couple.

He encouraged father and son to continue with their mysterious calculations and reminded them that they were excused all other duties.

The two looked for a suitable place to continue their watching and counting and there was no better place than the wall with Junior's plan of the village. Fred with the superior memory of his people knew how many days had passed since Junior had fetched him down from the Moyan home caves. He decided he needed to go back there and bring his calculations up to date only then would he be able to transfer everything down to the new wall.

Before he went, he said to Junior, "There's no lonesome pine to cast the sun's shadow for us, we need to make one down here. Go to Mike and get his help."

Junior scouted around and found a fallen tree, too big to be useful in construction. He showed Mike the tree and explained Fred's needs. He explained the tree could be used until a splinter of granite could be used to replace it.

Mike commandeered some labour and under his direction, the tree was trimmed and cut to a single trunk. Meanwhile, not too far from his wall, Junior found a clearing facing south, ideal for the new lonesome pine.

When Junior and a saddle-sore Fred came back, a pit was being dug. It was hard going in the stony ground, but after much complaining by the diggers, a hole as deep as a man is tall was ready.

Horses dragged the new lonesome pine to its new home and with leather ropes and wooden wedges, the tree pulled upright and the pit filled in. Fred was impressed once again by his son's abilities.

Chapter Sixteen
The Vornay Abandon the Eastern Plain

With the coming of spring, Buster of the Vornay and his Family and the representatives of the clans, Barry, Sam, Jock and Isla had negotiated their return journey through the mountains to the eastern plain. The river level was even lower than when Buster and family first came through. If Jude had been with them, which he wasn't, there was no chance of him coming to grief.

Spring had turned into early summer on the plain. The rains had failed, not for the first time, fodder for the animals was scarce and the plain started to resemble a dry semi-desert.

The Vornay families were in trouble. It was going to be a bleak summer never mind the next winter. Not enough fodder, not enough fuel and mindful of the Buster's expedition to the west, the families and their horses and flocks gradually moved towards the mountains, in the unspoken hope that salvation was beyond the mountains, and so it happened. The Buster group came out on to the eastern plain and almost immediately came across a young boy riding north searching for fresh pasture and after much hellos and out gaping at the visitors from the clans, he departed to spread the word of Buster's arrival.

The plight of the Vornay was such that a few days later and without exception, everyone met up with Buster to hear of their adventures on the other side of the mountains. Buster with the help of Lilly, Blake, Poppy and a few nods of agreement from Barry, Sam, Jock and Isla told of their Journey.

"First of all," Buster began and indicating the clans' men, "the people on the western side of the mountains are much like us, we have nothing to fear from them."

"In fact," Blake said, "they welcomed us, they showed us how they made these clothes and how to get rid of the beasties that make us scratch so."

He explained about the invention of needles and how they were able to build much bigger tents that wonder of wonders even had hearths inside them. Jock told them of the great plain.

"The grass is better, the herds roam in such great numbers, so many of them that hunting can provide all the meat we need."

Isla said, "Your way of using horses, sheep and goats is just wonderful. I can't think of why we have not done it ourselves."

Barry and Sam spoke next. Sam told them about the monsters from the south who had wiped out his family and virtually his whole clan.

"With our skills as hunters with the long spear and your expertise with horses, we should not fear them," Barry spoke with venom in his voice. "They killed my mother and father, we should attack and destroy them."

Saul, head of his family, spoke, "We lost a family to these southern barbarians. Yes! We should take the fight to them."

There was one major outcome from the meeting. The Vornay without a voice of dissent agreed that their future would look better in the western plain.

It was midsummer when the returning Vornay and their clan allies arrived in the eastern plain. In Buster's estimation, the Vornay people along with their animals would not reach the clans home turf before winter.

The logistic problem of moving all the families and their herds was tackled in two ways, an advanced party led by Kai travelling light, consisting of twenty mostly second sons, their wives and children along with Barry and Sam to lead the way. They took only their own horses and pack animals hoping to reach the clan before winter set in.

In the meantime, all the remaining Vornay prepared to abandon the eastern plain and if what they believed to be true of the western plain, they would overwinter in the more fertile western plain finding what shelter they could before moving on in the spring to join their advance party and the clans.

* * * *

In the long history of man, nature has conspired to kill him and make life at times almost impossible.

Fire, flood, drought, earthquake, tsunami, pestilence. But just once, nature was kind. It was late summer when the advance party reached the pass through the mountains, not a good time for a people and their horses to make the journey to new lands. The weather was good but there was a possibility that they would not reach the clans before the onset of winter. However, nature smiled on them. The drought that was causing so many problems, caused the river through the mountain to be mere shadow of its former self.

Two days later, the advance party entered the pass through the mountain and splashed through the reduced river until they, like the first expedition, encountered the steep cliffs and the flood plain and like the first expedition camped on the plain for the night and with plenty of driftwood, everyone had reasonably comfortable night. Next day at dawn, a recce party of four moved out and easily reached the first sandbar on horseback without getting wet, the next sandbar, which had nearly cost Jude his life, was reached with the water barely touching the horse's belly.

The riders trotted on to the end of the sandbar, entered shallow water and followed the river until it turned left. In front of them on their right was the other flood plain. The riders scrambled up onto it and rode for about a mile at which point the flood plain slopped gently down on to the great plain. The way through the mountain was made easy thanks to a benign nature.

The advance party reached the great plain two days later, only to discover what Buster had already said; there was plenty grass for horses and livestock.

"We should head south and west to join our clans before they go to the caves for the winter," said Barry

Day after day after day, the Vornay led by Barry and Sam headed for another historic meeting between two people and two cultures.

* * * *

One bright cold day, Sam recognised the tor where the two peoples had first encountered each other.

"Not far now, in less than a day we will be at our old summer camp and then it's up on to our home caves."

Kai was apprehensive of caves for generations, the Vornay had lived in tents on the plains with their animals. In winter, they moved to more sheltered areas where fodder had been stored. They had always lived in tents but in bad times in severe winters, the only heat source was a few animals brought inside. Living was harsh while the rest of the flocks were left to perish and provide food for the future.

When the advance party arrived at the now deserted summer camp, most of the tents had been dismantled. There was one exception, the Moree's tent built by Ash and Jean was still there. Sam and Barry looked in, astonished by its construction, and impressed by the improvements.

The arrival of the Vornay men, woman and children could hardly go on unnoticed.

When word reached the winter camp on the escarpment, building work stopped and everyone headed down to the plain streaming out in a long line towards the summer camp, but on approaching the horse people, they hung back and waited for leaders Mike, Ash, Murf and Star to go forward and there was Kai, Barry and Sam. They came forward with the leaders of the Vornay and again stilted introductions made with much over loud talking and touching of chests. This time, the meeting was smoothed by Barry and Sam able to speak Vornay and with months travelling together and thanks to that great memory of people at these times, many of the advance party could speak and understand clan at least a little.

The sudden arrival of the Vornay advance party was the biggest event of an already eventful year. Completion of the new winter quarters was not ready and with the autumn hunt, as dictated by Fred, just a few weeks away, the completion could not happen before the onset of winter.

The People of the clans had other ideas however, there was no way they were going back to their caves for the winter. The busy construction of the winter quarters became almost frenzied, the Vornay with their superior knowledge of horses completed the corrals and started pens for their herd animals due to arrive next year.

* * * *

On the other side of the mountains, the remainder of the Vornay families had come together, with horses and herd animals, slowly heading for the mountains and had reached the pass leading to the western plain. Like the advance party, nature smiled on them. The water in the river was at an all-time low. Nevertheless, the passage of over a hundred people including the elderly and children and nearly two-hundred horses and the herd animals, all that were left after the last poor years, was a massive undertaking and painfully slow. When they reached the first flood plain, there was not enough space for all.

Jock of the clan suggested that the horses and some families move beyond the two sandbars and on to the much larger second flood plain. Once achieved, there was room on the sand bar for an overnight camp.

Jock on the second sandbar led some of the Vornay men to western end and down onto the great plain. The horsemen were gladly able to confirm that the great plain was indeed more fertile than their former home and rode off to spread the word. John, immediately rode out to see with his own eyes. He surveyed the big flood plain and the great plain beyond and made his plans and on return to the families, held a meeting with their heads, he described the large flood plain and the easy access to the great plain and the caves in the cliff face and explained his plan,

"Winter approaches, we were going to winter on the new plain, my idea is we winter on the big flood plain, there is a huge amount of wood more than we ever saw, and there are caves which will need exploring."

Buster agreed and said, "We can build a barricade at the end to keep the animals on the flood plain."

"Talking of flood plains," someone said, "when the rains come, we could be flooded out."

John agreed and said, "We may have to evacuate in a hurry."

Buster pointed out, "The rains have been failing for years, there's a good chance we will be alright."

They agreed, work started on the barricade to keep the animals off the plain. The huge task was of collecting wood from both flood plains and storing them in caves, an even bigger task was collecting and storing fodder from the great plain. Horsemen went out to find the herd animals and returned dragging several auroch, not enough to last all winter. It was not enough and it appeared that the plains animals had started their annual migration.

Things were bad on the other side of the mountain range but the situation on this side the great plain was no better. In fact, they were worse. The horse people were familiar with their old territory and had long established the places to shelter from the worse that winter could bring but west of the mountains they were in unfamiliar territory, the vast western plain appeared to go on for ever and seemed to offer little shelter.

The large flood plain in the mountain offered the best place to overwinter.

The leaders of the families along with everyone else knew that there was not going to be enough food to last. The prospect of sacrificing some of their horses to survive hardly bared thinking about.

* * * *

Kai of the Vornay advance party, now settled in and helping with the clan's winter quarters on the escarpment was nevertheless worried about the main body of Vornay, had they negotiated the mountain pass? Had they found shelter on the great plain, did they have enough food and fodder? He voiced his concerns to all Vornay and clan alike.

Mike, mindful of a journey he made bringing food to the Moray in the time of their need, a time which seemed so long ago suggested to Kai that he should head back to the mountains and search for his people.

"Take as many horses as you need, we have, thanks to you, plenty and more than plenty dried meat, we have salt from the sea and we can spare a few dried root herbs and berries."

Kai and five of the men from the advance party loaded their horses and a long line of pack horses loaded with as much supplies as the clan could spare. They headed out towards hopefully the rest of their people.

Buster the first of the Vornay to cross the great plain had taken six of ten days to find and meet the clans.

Kai without family and driven by a sense of urgency pushed on day after day. He had another advantage to Buster's journey; that terrific memory of all people at that time, he navigated a more direct route avoiding time wasting detours.

Within less than three of ten days, he sighted the mountains but as they approached, the weather broke, the sky darkened. The wind had become colder as the days passed, it turned bitter and the first flurries of snow blew in their faces.

Increasing wind and snow had now turned into a full blizzard, still no sign of their people. The riders reached the river that flowed through the mountain and with the river on their right, they set off blindly towards what they knew to be the large flood plain protected by cliffs on the left and with the river on their right. There was no shelter on the great plain, their only hope was to reach the mountain.

Kai was worried where were his people. Had they decided not to migrate? Had they been attacked by the murderers from the south? His immediate worry was about himself and the rest of the party. If shelter wasn't found soon, they would be in trouble. Men and horses could not survive in these conditions, their only hope was the large flood plain.

The ground rose gently towards the flood plain but as the riders approached the top and the entrance to the flood plain, they were confronted by a barrier of wood and river debris, obviously man made.

Darren was eight, still a child but soon to be a boy, and in just a few years a man, but he was still young enough to cheek his mother and as punishment, was sent in the cold and snow from his warm family tent to check the western barrier and repair it if needed.

Kai thought he saw movement on the other side of the fence and shouted out. A head appeared on top of the barrier and Darren shouted, "Uncle Kai!"

He started to make a gap to let men and horses through, he made a triumphant return leading Kai's horse. However, he was brought down with a bang when he was sent back to repair the gap he had made.

The Vornay didn't like caves but there was one cave that could accommodate everyone and everyone was glad to get shelter from what was now a blizzard and hear all the news. The pack horses were led into an adjacent cave alongside the flock animals to be unloaded. Then everyone adjourned to the larger cave to hear the advance party's story and what a story Kai was going to tell as he and the rest of the men came into the cave to join the families. They took off their fur wraps, everyone gaped in amazement, even in the poor light in the cave, the new arrivals from the clans were dressed like the clan in trousers and fur lined smocks. Their feet wrapped in fur-lined wraps, shaped sewn and held together by leather ties far superior to the winter attire worn by the people.

Kai was a great speaker and held the horse people enthralled with his story of the people of the clans. "They have just recently moved to tents from their caves and their tents are better than ours." He went on to explain how they could sew many hides together thanks to their needles.

Kai went on, "Unlike us, they are now all living in one place. They have, in just a few years, moved from caves on the great escarpment to tents on the great plain. Now they have moved back on to the escarpment to the shelter of the trees for the winter."

Someone said, "Back to their caves?"

"Oh no!!! Now they're building with not just hides, they are using wood and dung as well," Kai went on to tell the families how Buster in anticipation of the main Vornay's arrival had supervised and helped build corrals and pens. "The clans have left space for all our tents but, when you see their tents some with clay, dung and wooden walls, I know you will want to build ours in the same way. When we left, they were building a meeting place that will be able to hold many families."

People cried, "Impossible, no one can build a tent to hold that many families."

"Yes, they can, I have seen the pictures."

He told the families of the flat cliff face where Junior, a man of the clan, had marked out the whole area in pictures.

"I have looked at the wall and I can see where our animals will be kept, where we can build our tents and where the clans' people have built their tents. It even shows where their middens are, latrines paths and the stream that runs through the area are all shown."

The families were fascinated, most barely understood what he was saying.

"The clans have much to offer if we stay with them or at least nearby, but we also have much to offer them. For meat they had to go out on the great plain to hunt and until we arrived, they had to do it on foot. We've given them horses to make hunting easier and if we can keep some sheep and goats through this winter, they can benefit from our skills in keeping flocks."

Saul, a family head, agreed, "Together we will be stronger if the tribe from the south attacks us."

Kai said, "Mike has thought of that and in the summer, he intends to send men to spy on them. He intended to send men out two summers ago but got caught up with all the changes. I say we join them."

With that, the meeting ended and everyone was glad to get out of the cave and back to their tents to sit out the blizzard, and so the Vornay with the extra supplies brought by Kai endured the long cold winter on the flood plain.

Chapter Seventeen
A Hard Winter

On the escarpment, enough work had been done to allow the clans to endure the winter without having to return to their home caves. The corrals for the horses were not complete. Some animals were penned in the old Mizuki caves, winter supplies, wood and fodder were stored in another.

The snows came late but when it did, it came with a vengeance; the blizzard lasted a week. It seemed to be permanently dark, visibility was just a few paces, most tents re-enforced with extra hides and wooden poles turf and stone weights stood up to the weather but not all, several collapsed. The clans' leaders were forced from their warm tents to organise some families to double up, tempers were lost and once again, firm leadership won the day. Without the strong presence of the leaders, there was a possibility that the whole clan structure and the beginnings of a nation might collapse.

Mike calmed things down by pointing out that the collapsed tents were just in a too exposed position and the collapse was not due to poor building workmanship. Strictly speaking, this wasn't the complete truth but not only was Mike a strong leader, he was also a diplomat.

With the passing of the blizzard, the weather turned exceptionally cold, windless blue skies, heavy frosts, the lying snow froze, but life went on double wrapped in furs. The men of the clans went on with what business they could. Horses fed and watered. Repairs, reinforcements and rebuilding of homes made. Boys were sent out to search for extra firewood to add to the stockpile. The primitive and fragile clay pots, which had become so common because of their ease of production, became precious; no new ones made until the winter was over.

Once a day under the supervision of the leaders' wives, frozen dried meat and some greens were distributed to the wives of the families. Girls collected and melted snow for water.

The winter had been hard on Fred's calculations of the advancing year, he hardly ever saw the sun or moon. After his and Junior's visit to the cave by the sea and his counting the days on the new wall and marking them up, what was next? He remembered from that visit, the huge number of vertical lines in groups of four with a single horizontal through each group. It didn't take much imagination to realise these mysterious people counted in fives. It was Junior's input that put him on the right track

One bleak winter day, the two of them were looking at Fred's marking of the days.

"With everything that has been happening, I have lost track of the year now? Will I be able to find midsummer?"

Junior, no longer a boy at the age of fourteen, he was a man. He had seen death, and was soon to be a father.

"Dad," he said, "you have marked on the wall one mark for every day, we should be able to count the days from last midsummer to last midwinter and on to this midsummer."

Fred moaned, "How can I make sense of all these lines?"

Junior looked at all his father's lines grouped in fives, just like the sea cave except something was missing and thinking back to his two visits to the cave, he realised what it was. "The lines mean days, yes?"

"Yes."

"But in the cave, the lines were under the moons."

Fred saw it straight away, "There were so many lines between one new moon and the next, how can we count them? We will have to go back to the cave to see."

Junior replied, "We don't need to. I remember, between one moon and the next, there were five lines and another five that makes ten then there five more lines and another five that makes another ten and the same again. Between one new moon and the next, there are three tens of days."

Fred said, "If I go back to when I started on this wall last midsummer and count three tens of my day-marking, that will be the next new moon and another three tens to the next new moon. I know that there are ten new moons and another two between one midsummer and the next, and we have the new lonesome pine to tell us exactly when midsummer day arrives."

In the winter camp of the clan in mid-February, father and son started to calculate when the next midsummer would occur.

In the clan like other winters, children were born, some died, a few older people died some not so old. People didn't notice but there were fewer deaths that winter than usual. The clans were healthier and better fed, hygiene completely unknown a few years ago was a big part of this change. The scourge of summer biters and more importantly the lice and flees that had previously been taken for granted had almost been eliminated.

With the clans all living together, a gradual change in leadership had taken place. Mike, known to be fair as well as strong, took on the mantle of leadership. Ash, Murf and Star slotted in harmoniously as his deputies and if the truth be known, they were glad to have the office but not the responsibility. One of Mike's worries was that he had failed to send an expedition south to recce the tribe responsible for the deaths in both clans and Vornay. With the coming of horses, he resolved to mount the agreed expedition in the spring and then remembering that the rest of the Vornay families might be arriving in the spring, he put off thoughts of an expedition again and hoped he wouldn't regret it.

The winter slowly headed to spring, Mike went around to Fred's tent. He wasn't there. June pointed him in the direction of the old Mizuki caves.

"Junior and Fred spend a lot of time up there making marks on the wall beside the pictures of our village. I don't see the point."

Mike trudged up the slope and found them gazing at a wall partially covered with lines and curves. "You want to know when the plain's animals will arrive?" said Fred. "Well, we were just working on that very problem."

"Can you give me answer?"

Junior said, "Yes, in just a few moments."

Mike didn't want to break up their work so although he was the leader of all the people of the clans, he trudged back down the hill to fetch Ash Murf and Star.

When everyone assembled, Fred started to explain the meaning of all the lines and curves carved on to the wall.

"You see, we need to find midsummer and midwinter because after these days the days they will get longer after midwinter and after midsummer, the days will start to get shorter. The first time we measured the shadows, the animals started their journey south four new moons and eight days after midsummer."

"Yes," said Murf, "but when will they arrive this spring?" Mike shushed him and indicated to Fred to carry on.

"When the herds came back in the spring it was four new moons and a few days after midwinter." Fred stopped and drew breath. "This year, we have a problem. The weather has been so bad with endless cloudy skies, we have lost touch with the moon." Murf groaned.

Junior took over.

"All is not lost, we now know that between one midsummer and the next or between one midwinter and the next there are ten new moons and another two new moons, and a few days."

Quick on the uptake, Ash said, "That's what all these lines and curves are for."

Fred explained, "Every line means a day and every curve a new moon. See how we have arranged the days under each new moon, there are ten days and another ten days and another ten under each new moon."

Murf again asked, "When will the herds return?"

Murf seemed to be the only one who couldn't see where these conversations were going.

Mike went over to the wall.

"What does this mean?" He pointed to a circle beside a new moon, "That was the day of midsummer."

Mike walked along the wall to another circle beside a new moon.

"This circle is smaller, that must mean midwinter."

Fred and Junior were delighted and proud that Mike was able to read their wall.

Mike went back to midsummer and counted the new moons, there were six, he started to count the new moons from midwinter until the marked days ran out, pointing to the last vertical line Mike said, "This is today, yes!"

Fred and Junior were delighted, you could say they were over the moon.

Murf had lost interest but Ash said, "And you think the herds return as usual."

Murf came out of his boredom and said, "All these tens are confusing, I can't follow them. We have words for one to ten, why don't we make words for numbers more than ten?"

There was a stunned silence, the idea was almost too much to think about. Fred shouted, "Why didn't I think of that?"

He calmed down and said, "Junior and I will spend time on that."

The meeting was over, the clan leaders went down to the almost finished meeting tent and shooed everyone away and made plans for the first spring hunt.

Mike remembered a conversation he had with Buster. He said, "The Vornay not only have their horses, they have other animals they keep for meat. At the start of winter they slaughter some, but they also keep some alive for the next year." Thinking further, "Buster said in bad weather they bring the animals inside their tents to keep them alive and their bodies help keep the tents warm." The thoughts of animals in their tents didn't go down well, but the idea of a constant supply of fresh meat was appealing.

* * * *

Preparations for the spring hunt went ahead. With horses, the hunters were confident of success.

The horses had been corralled all winter. They had been exercised regularly as advised by their new eastern friends, but men and horses were glad to go out and run on the great plain.

Chapter Eighteen
Start of the Vornay's Great Trek

On the flood plain, all the families had endured the winter. Again the rains east of the mountain range had failed and as a result, the river even in early march was very low. When the weather allowed, everyone went out on to the great plain that would soon be their new home. It was obvious that this plain was more fertile. Even in early march, their animals were able to graze on the winter grass, and with a sense of rising excitement, the Vornay prepared to head west and meet the people they had heard so much about.

John as head of the senior family urged caution, "It's too early to leave the shelter of the mountain. We need to wait until we can be sure the weather won't close in." It was agreed, however, that Buster and his family including Jude should leave as soon as possible to tell the clans of the imminent arrival of the whole Vornay nation.

Nine days later, Buster set out across the great plain to renew acquaintance with his friends in the clans.

Ten days after that, the families started to dismantle their tents and pack them for the longest journey that they would ever make.

The Vornay were impressed by this plain even in early spring, the grass was more verdant than the grass on the eastern side of the mountains. There were groves of trees far more than they had ever seen. In the distance, herds of animals, some never seen before. There were small herds of horses and, as Buster had first observed, they seemed unafraid and curious of their domesticated cousins.

However, progress across the great plain was slow. The remaining livestock had to be continuously driven on as they kept stopping to investigate a new patch of grass. Kai was able to guide the trek avoiding some of the worst areas.

However, unbroken ground, young children, old people and heavily laden packhorses did not help. Nevertheless, without the horse, it would have been a sorry and much diminished Vornay that would have arrived to meet their new allies.

Day after day, the long column of people and horses and domestic animals made their way west.

* * * *

Buster led his group at a much faster pace. They reached the clans' summer camp by his calculations in ten days and ten days and one five days.

There was only one tent left, the original tent built by Ash. Even after a harsh winter it still stood but was in imminent danger of falling down.

All the other tents now dismantled and moved to the clans' winter quarters.

Buster looked west to the escarpment and saw men on horseback heading towards them.

"A welcome committee I hope," he said out loud. He was not wrong, Mike greeted Buster as a long-lost friend and escorted Buster and his family to the escarpment and to the new home of the clans.

Mike said, "Let me show you your new home."

Building work started in late summer had continued through the winter as weather allowed but with the coming of spring and over a hundred workers, strong leadership and Junior's plan to follow, the people of the clans were well on their way to building a village. Junior's plan called for a central area similar to the home caves. In the middle of which was the half-built leaders' meeting tent.

Radiating outwards were the dwellings of the clans. Their new homes had progressed beyond just animal hide covering; wood, dried mud and animal dung were also incorporated/ no longer did the people shelter behind stone walls surrounding their hearth in wet, cold, dank caves. Now each family lived in not quite a tent and not quite a hut but something in between; much easier to keep warm with a central fire in every tent.

Buster and his family were impressed at the progress made by the people of the clans, who worked together in a way far superior to the loose collaboration between the Vornay.

Mike said, "Come and see the picture of our homes, Junior will show you."

Junior took the Vornay family to his wall drawing.

The boy in Junior was long gone and with his and his dad's superior knowledge of numbers, the seasons and increasingly new words to add to the people's language and marriage to Sasha, he had become a confident and respected member of the Moyan clan.

In fact, some of his contemporaries were sometimes a bit difficult with him but he still had his old friends from his expedition to the sea. Jim, Wally, Alan from the Moyan and the rest of the boys, now men from the other clans especially Sam and Barrie who would soon be arriving with the Vornay people at the end of their long migration.

Stopping in front of the cliff face, adorned with the plan of the clans' new winter home. To the left was what was now a calendar although Fred, Junior and possibly Mike were the only ones who could read it. Junior gave his now honed and practised lecture.

Buster and his family had never seen anything like it. Junior was proud of his creation. "Here is our meeting area with the clan leaders' meeting tent in the middle."

He then pointed out the hut/tents of the families, "I have stepped out the whole area. Each family's hut will be ten paces from the next. There is the area where you can build your tents, there is plenty of room."

Mike interrupted, "Your area is more sheltered. These symbols mean trees. See how close together they are and on the other side of the trees the corral for the horses is nearly finished, further on down you can build places to keep these animals that you are bringing."

Buster hummed.

"What's wrong?"

He said, "We prefer to keep our animals closer in case of wolves."

On the escarpment, there were no wolves although on the plain, they had been seen, however, Mike agreed to bring the animal pens nearer the Vornay tents.

Later that day, the Buster family moved to what would be their new home and as they erected their tents, Buster thought that not all his people would want to live on the escarpment. He suspected that some, even most, would remain on the plain and resume their nomadic life.

Mike appeared and invited everyone to the central meeting place to eat.

"When we were building our new homes, the woman banded together to cook for everyone but now we have started to go back to our old ways. Every family cooks for themselves but as our guests, what is ours is yours.

Because of you and your horses the clans no longer feel afraid of starvation in winter."

Later, Ash, Murf and Star joined them and the talk was of the imminent arrival of the Vornay. Buster said, "I doubt they will be half way here by now even with the guidance of Sam and Barry. Would it be possible for pack horses with food and even some clothes to follow on?"

The answer was yes, of course.

Mike realised the importance of this first meeting with the whole Vornay people, everyone's future wellbeing and security depended on the coming together of the two people. In private, he expressed this to Ash, Murf and Star. The result was that a few days later, Buster led the biggest train of horses that could be spared all loaded with dried meat and what other supplies and clothing that could be spared or impounded departed the escarpment, so much in fact that food for the clans was becoming short.

The followers were pressed into service. As ex-hunters this was something that they were very happy to do to regain some of the status of their former life now made possible for them with the advent of the horse.

* * * *

Buster, as the lead in the expedition and with unerring accuracy, headed north and east and within ten days and five days had a joyous reunion with his people. The arrival of fresh supplies could not have come at a better time, morale and food was low.

Mike would have been gratified had he been there as both clan and Vornay met together in an almost carnival atmosphere.

Buster, Barry and Sam, and a few others were much in demand as translators. The latest tent designed for summer on the plain erected and the power of the needle again shown to be a showstopper. There was not enough clan clothes to go around but quite a few lucky Vornay swanked it in front of their peers.

* * * *

Robin belonged to the clan Rabeel as a hunter. He had witnessed the deaths and injuries of some of his friends, he had stood steadfast with his fellow hunters as they faced many dangerous situations, not least an injured Bison as they closed in for the final kill. Today, he faced a new challenge, a little Vornay girl no more than five years approached him. She was holding a new born lamb and offered it up to Robin to hold. In all his life, Robin had only handled dead animals and here was a little girl doing something he had never dreamed of doing, holding a live animal.

The girl held out the lamb, Robin hesitated and looked around, both clan and Vornay looked on with interest. Gingerly, he held out both hands and lifted the lamb to his chest, the big brave clansman would never have admitted it, but he liked it.

In the years to come, he witnessed death and slaughter of domestic animals and humans. It was necessary for the continued existence of the people, but he never forgot that little lamb and the way it looked up at him.

Buster and his family, Lilly, Jude, Blake and Poppy elected to stay and guide the people to the clans. The senior family of the Vornay, John guided by Barry and Sam set out ahead of the main body. John was eager to see where his people would be moving to. Barry and

Sam were eager to get home and pushing on as fast as they could. Following what was becoming a recognised trail, they reached the escarpment in ten days.

Mike as always rode out to greet them and escort them to the clans' winter home and again more of the Vornay people were more than impressed with the homes of the clans laid out on a plateau on an escarpment surrounded by more trees than John had ever seen in his entire life.

Formalities over, the new arrivals were shown Junior's wall drawings of the clans' village.

John said to Mike, "These are your winter homes and that in the summer you move out on to the plain?" Mike agreed.

John said, "We live on our plain in the summer and in the winter, we go up to the hills and canyons to ride out the bad weather. That is not much different to you. Tell me what this plain is like in winter?"

"The wind, snow and ice come straight down from the north. When the weather is bad, life on the plain is impossible. The trees on the escarpment offer shelter, in fact, we intend to build walls to offer even more shelter."

"My thoughts, I will talk to the other families, we may live on these plains of yours near your home but I suspect that in winter, we may join you if that is acceptable."

"Yes, of course. My hope is that you all join with us and that one day between us, we will overcome our enemy in the south."

One day, two riders arrived, Blake and Poppy announcing the imminent arrival of the main body of the Vornay People. A day later, gradually on the horizon, a long black ribbon appeared. As it came closer, the ribbon was more like a river, and at last coming into focus, the people of the Vornay arrived at their new home.

Mike and John were prepared and had planned for their arrival. Central communal cooking introduced at the height of construction of the village and now abandoned as it took shape; the people going back to family cooking.

Communal cooking was again introduced, with most families supplying a member, a son, a daughter, a grandmother or new wife to a son pressed into service.

Mike oversaw the selection of 'volunteers' and with his unfailing wisdom, achieved this with very little complaint. Junior's planned meeting area turned out to accommodate just about everyone and his father's meeting with Mike produced the building of more fire pits.

Fred was getting used to working with numbers and by all accounts, the Vornay numbered in the many ten. Possibly ten of tens and maybe more.

Fred looked at the communal cooking facilities that had fed the clans during the building of their village. One clan numbered ten and ten and ten and ten and there were four clans. Fred increasingly involved in numbers saw at once that the fire pits were insufficient to feed the clan and the Vornay.

He said to Mike, "When they arrive, we will have to eat separately."

Mike would have none of it. "When our new friends arrive, at least for the first time, we will all eat together."

And so, the fire pits under Fred's direction were extended.

The arrival of Blake and Poppy started the preparations. When the long column was spotted, the line of fire pits, extended on the recommendation of Fred and had been kept burning, were allowed to damp down, stones added. The hot stones would cook the meat.

When the stones were deemed hot enough, sticks were used to remove them and place them on an adjacent fire while the embers of the fire were removed. The hot stones were now returned to the pit and covered with grass and leaves.

The meat was now added, and bedded down with more grass and leaves and then the whole pit was covered with soil. The greenery in the pit containing the water turned to steam keeping the meat moist. Steam escaping from the pit was patted down with more earth.

Chapter Nineteen
The Vornay Arrive

The arrival of the horse people was a strangely quiet affair, animals driven into the prepared pens. Horses were unloaded, corralled and fed. John had advised the clans on the domestic animals' requirements, something Mike had not even thought.

The Vornay tasks completed and as directed made their way to the centre of the village. As they filed in, they could hardly believe their eyes. The clan leaders' meeting hut was sat on slightly higher ground and was bigger than anything they had ever seen. Mike, Ash and Murf and their wives accompanied by John and his wife stood outside, ready to welcome them.

Every one of the clans who could be there was there, mostly on the periphery of the meeting area. A few clan members and a few Vornay had met before and human nature being what it was, sought out and greeted each other. But most clan and Vornay were strangers to each other. As a result, the whole assembly stood quietly; no one knew what to do next.

Mike and John were about to go into a welcome speech when the smell of cooked food drifted over every one. The food from the fire pits was ready and couldn't be delayed any longer, a line of 'volunteers' came down bearing the food, tree bark platters, clay pots, bowls and platters. The 'volunteers' under Fred's direction had resorted to raiding their families' huts to get enough bowls and platters to serve everyone.

Mike, ever resourceful, encouraged the clan to move in to the meeting area and greet their new neighbours. The area was packed. clan and Vornay alike, shared plates, pots and platters.

There is no better way for strangers to meet and join than sharing food. The 'volunteers' resorted to snatching empty plates and running uphill to refill them. Children were on duty to pass animal skin pouches of water as they ran to the stream. Vornay children went and helped.

The quiet, subdued meeting place gradually started to get a bit noisy, again there was much loudly beating of chests and the saying of names and as the noise increased, laughter heard above the increasing hubbub.

Mike and John never made their welcome speeches. As time went on and no time to erect tents for the whole Vornay people and darkness approaching, the clan invited new friends to their homes, gradually the meeting area emptied. Mike and John and the welcoming committee were at first mortified that events had side-lined them and stole their thunder but, at the same time glad that the meeting of the two had come off with such success.

* * * *

The next day, the heads of the Vornay families met to decide where to pitch their tents and it was agreed that as before, they wanted to live on the plain. Their former homes separated over a large area, necessary because of the poor and sparse vegetation for their domestic animals but on this more fertile plain, they erected their tents virtually in sight of each other with the option of moving to the more sheltered escarpment in winter.

133

The two peoples started to settle down together. Hunting the plain's animals became a joint venture. There was a surplus of food due to overkill of animals because of the high demand for their skins needed for clothing and building material.

The horse people's tents on the plain started to resemble the more sophisticated clan homes, which had started to look more like huts than tents.

Life for both peoples started to settle down that summer, more horses captured and broken. The clans were fascinated by domestic animals, goats' and sheep milk unheard of by the clans was only upstaged and much prized by cheese.

The Vornay for their part could hardly credit the newly required horsemanship of the clan hunters, and their support when bringing down animals.

The tree covered escarpment in turn provided fresh deer meat, roots, vegetables, edible leaves and much more that had been lacking in their diet. Clay pots and bowls were a wonder but most of all, they admired their clothes.

The weeks passed, spring had turned into summer and was heading towards the clans' summer festival now started on midsummer's day. Thanks to Fred's calculations, this year's event promised to be the biggest and most spectacular ever seen as the combined population was over four hundred, not that anyone was counting simply because they couldn't count. There were two exceptions to this, Fred and Junior.

Fred had been counting the new moons but he discovered that on midsummer's day, the moon would be in a different phase from last year. Counting the new moons was a help but not accurate to forecast midsummer and midwinter, he came to realise the way to do it was to count the number of days between one midsummer and the next and he would have to rely on the lonesome pine.

Chapter Twenty
The Summer Festival

Preparations for the summer festival and the clans' move to the plain for the summer started ten days before a new moon, and it would be another new moon and another ten and ten days before midsummer. Soon, a new village started to spring up. It was within sight of the nearest Vornay tents with a stream running down from the escarpment between the two camps, nearby were two tors separated by a few tens of spaces. The Vornay had already fenced off the gap with wood between them for their domestic animals. They delighted in the abundance of wood in their new home. Unlike their former plain where wood was scarce so much so that soon they would catch up or even overtake their woodworking skills over the clans.

There was one skill in which the clans excelled over the Vornay; flint knapping. A skill essential in processing everything from wood to meat to fish to bone to hide. In the Vornay's former home, flint was less abundant but still necessary in their everyday life, but here in their new home range, flint was everywhere.

The day of the midsummer festival dawned bright and warm with great excitement within the clans, less so among the Vornay, they knew more or less what to expect but knowing and experiencing are two different things.

Traditionally, the woman of one clan took it in turns to cook for the other clans, due to the greater numbers, a different plan was called for. Again, family cooking was abandoned in favour of communal cooking

Mike's leadership again came to the fore, he selected 'volunteers'; John did likewise. The 'volunteers' were grouped into fours and would provide food for everyone. While only "volunteering" for one day in four, everyone was able to enjoy the festivities.

With the huge number of people to feed, Mike was unsure if the cooks were up to the job. It would be a disaster if not enough food was prepared and with the lines of fire pits, spits on cooking fires, mounds of pottery, it seemed too much for a people who normally counted in tens.

Fred was in on the conversation when Mike expressed his doubts. Fred and his son were the only clan members who could count beyond ten. He had determined that the only way for sure to determine midsummers' day was to count the number of days between one midsummer and the next, with the shadow of the lonesome pine to confirm his calculations.

The task was not as difficult as he first thought. Two midsummers ago, he started counting the days. He marked the days in group of ten on his wall. When he had ten tens, he invented a symbol for ten tens. He discovered that he had three symbols for ten tens and an incomplete ten of tens between one midsummer and the next. He improved on this by counting between midsummer and midwinter.

One benefit of all Fred's efforts in counting apart from predicting the movements of the herds was to advise the 'volunteers' on how much food was needed to feed everyone.

"One meal," he said to Emily, one of the 'volunteers'. "How much food would you prepare for one person, can you show me?"

Emily took a clay platter, and put meat and some greens.

"Can you agree that is enough for one person?"

Fred did agree and took a bark platter and made up a meal of fish.

"I would say this is about right for another meal," Emily agreed.

Fred went away and with the help of Junior, calculated how much food was needed to feed every one for one festive meal.

Junior already knew how many clans' people there were. However, at his dad's insistence and as an exercise in counting, Junior calculated all the people of the clans numbered the symbol for ten of tens and another ten of tens, and another ten of tens and six tens.

Fred calculated the Horse people numbered just less of the symbol for ten of tens, he went back to Emily and the rest of the 'volunteers', and calculated how many fire pits could make ten festive meals. It became apparent that the existing fire pits and cooking fires were insufficient, and at Mike's and Fred's orders, even more pits were dug and prepared. Children and the young spent days collecting firewood.

The day started early for the 'volunteers'. The first order was the morning feast, no mean feat for the 'volunteers' who had to cater for nearly five-hundred.

They had in fact started the day before, lighting the fire pits and starting the cooking process, conscripting the children to carry down even more wood and bark from the escarpment and adding to the huge amount already collected. They brought more turf, grasses, leaves then set out to 'borrow' more pottery and strip more tree bark for platters.

The clans were now, whenever possible, hanging meat before cooking. Hunting using horses had changed their hand to mouth existence making this possible. In addition to meat cooked in the fire pits, mounds of fish were laid out on strips of bark and alongside the fish, piles of vegetables, roots and shoots ready to be steamed in the pits, and above all, a huge mound of meat awaited including sheep and goat's.

Dawn saw the clans eager to begin the festival, assembled in their meeting area outside the great hut of the leaders. Mike along with Ash, Murf and Star came out to welcome everyone. He wanted to make a speech to start the festival off but one look at the crowd, impatient to be off and celebrate, made him change his mind, and as with all great leaders, he went with the flow and led the people in one long procession down the well-trodden path from the escarpment to the plain.

The Horse people seeing the procession formed their own procession and made their way to the start of the festivities. The two groups merged and everyone moved towards the delicious smell emanating from the cooking area, where the 'volunteers' waited apprehensively. No one had ever cooked so much food for so many before but thanks to the direction of Mike, John and Fred, the festival got off to a great start with more than enough food and plenty left over for snacks before the next big meal in the evening.

It took the 'volunteers' hours to feed everyone, huge queues formed, some people becoming impatient. Mike, Ash, Murf and Star mingled with the crowd. Mike joked that if they were tired of waiting, maybe they could go and help the 'volunteers', they were no takers.

John helped. He was bringing his horses to meet with the clans' horses for the children's race when he diverted his string of horses to the waiting crowd. He rode his horse up and down, and was a great distraction for the impatient queue. Most clans' people had little contact with horses, especially woman. They were both fascinated and frightened at the same time but not the children, they knew no fear and broke ranks to get close to the horses.

In the queue were Willy and Alice with their new daughter, Ava.

Spotting Willy, John invited him on to a horse then invited Alice and baby on another.

Willy remembering his first meeting with horses and his initial fear, he dismounted and called for volunteers to ride one, "Don't let the men have all the fun, look at Alice and Ava, she loves horses, come on and try riding a horse."

Out from the queue, a few younger women hesitantly came forward. John seized the initiative and with no great difficulty, ordered his compatriots to assist the young women. And who would not want to help a girl on to a horse and lead her round the cooking area, sometimes more than once. Relationships were made that day as a young man held out his arms to help a young woman off a horse as she allowed herself to fall into his arms.

The distraction of the hungry impatient crowd took off. Clans' horses were brought down to assist, hunters and followers called on their woman, folk friends and children to admire their horsemanship inviting them to join them on their horses for a short trip around the area.

Mike and John stood and watched as the first festive meal of the day starting out with crowds waiting to be fed, ended with the 'volunteers' shouting for customers.

* * * *

The summer festival lasted three days. The first day was for feasting and wandering about to see what had changed since last year, it ended with another festive meal.

The next day, new 'volunteers' laboured in the cooking area while all the latest technology was put on show. Clothes of the latest design were paraded, the latest developments in curing and tanning leather were on show.

Lessons in pottery manufacture, given especially on the new method of firing the clay. The previous way to fire a pot was similar to the fire pits used to cook meat, the pots and plates were useable but still too fragile. Time and again, broken pots thrown on to a fire had proved to be even harder when recovered, it seemed the hotter the fire, the stronger the pot or plate and different people were experimenting with new ways to fire a pot.

Demonstrations in new construction methods of the clans' tents were shown, wood and clay were increasingly being used as construction material, the jaw bones of animals both big and small could be sharpened to strip bark.

Flint axes previously held in the hand had gotten bigger, many now had a shaft.

It seemed there was nothing new under the sun today, house-building developments always have a show home and so it was thousands of years ago. Ash and his wife, Jean of the Moree came good again and with the help of his clan, Ash built the biggest, the finest and sturdiest structure ever seen on the great plain.

Posts had been dug into the ground, a first in the clan. People came and looked and wandered away. The posts became the supports for wooden walls filled in with clay and dung. Bigger central posts were dug that would eventually hold the hide roof, the hides of many animals provided that roof.

There was, of course, the now familiar central fire pit. But new to the clan were two curtained off rooms at the back of the tent which were to be used as sleeping areas. When it was completed, everyone came to inspect, gawk and admire Ash and Jean's new home.

Clansmen, on viewing these private areas, thought it a great idea.

Before the third day began, a new batch of 'volunteers' started preparations for the biggest day of the festival.

Today for the first time, the day would be competition and race day. By now, Mike and everyone else in the clans realised that their future was tied up with horses, most didn't think of it like that but Mike did. He was determined to involve as many of the clan as possible while, of course, the Vornay needed no prompting.

The morning began with a meal as usual for everyone and by now, delivered much more efficiently.

The first race of the day was for young children holding tightly on to a travois with the rider, usually dad. The race was three circuits round a specially made track, the winner receiving a prize.

The Vornay were next to show their expertise, five riders rode out at breath-taking speed towards five girls standing in an extended line. They raced around and around the line, the audience had never seen such speed. It seemed impossible that man and horse could move so fast. The riders slowed, formed a line, and stopped, each rider facing a girl. The distance between riders and girls was ten of ten paces.

The hubbub of the onlookers quietened, the girls stood perfectly still, the riders and their horses were completely still; not even a hoof pawing the ground. Suddenly and seemingly without a word of command, the riders took off at breakneck speed towards the line, only slowing at the very last minute, each rider leaned low and with an out stretched arm, scooped a girl and slung her over his horse and accelerated away towards the escarpment.

It was some time before the riders and their captives appeared back onto the plain.

Next, hunters showed their newly acquired riding skills. Ten and ten of children ran on to the plain. They pretended to be wild animals and spreading out, they ran around with great enthusiasm, arms outstretched and making strange animal noises.

The picture of the children running around and making noises delighted the onlookers.

From behind the cooking area, ten and another ten hunters raced out on to the plain. Splitting in two, they surrounded the children. They came to a halt, turned inwards, slowly advancing, herding the children into an increasingly smaller area. Unknown to the audience, a previously rehearsed play unfolded, three children broke free and raced passed the riders in a bid for freedom. Instantly, three riders wheeled after them and scooped them up and deposited them among their friends before herding them into the crowd.

In the evening after a last meal, there followed some wild storytelling, mostly by hunters, and again the story of the Vornay and their epic journey through the mountains to the east, especially Jude's brush with death.

Gradually as the light faded, the people started to wend their way home.

Chapter Twenty-One
First Expedition South

After the summer festival, the next big event would be the annual hunt. While still vital in the life of the clans, the horse and travois had changed the operation. No longer did the herds come to them, now the hunters went to them and drove the herds towards the killing zones.

On the last evening of the festival while people socialised and told their stories, Mike called the leaders and senior men of the people to a meeting. It was the first summer festival of the two peoples. It had been a great success. As they all sat outside Ash and Jean's great tent, and chewed the fat, Mike let the conversation run as they looked back on the last few days and with the odd prompt from him, the talk looked forward to next year's festival, suggestions made on how to improve things.

Mike cleared his throat, conversation died as everyone looked at Mike.

"The reason I asked you here is to talk about something we have all been ignoring. What do we do about the attacks from the people of the south?"

John said, "When we were attacked, these killers were on foot."

Mike agreed, "As were the attackers on us, they don't appear to use horses, this is our advantage."

Ash suggested, "We send a small party south to find out more."

Star said, "If they don't use horses, we can't let them see ours. We will have to be careful."

Helped by mugs of 'herbal' tea, the talks went on well into the night, lit by a full moon and a campfire.

A consensus was reached, each of the four clans would supply two hunters each, the Vornay would supply two. These men were the nearest that the two peoples had, that came close to warriors. If the truth be known, they had no word for warrior or in fact war.

The next day, preparations were made. Word went out, who would be selected to make the dangerous journey into the unknown. Volunteers were not needed, clansmen came forward immediately, Jock, the young hunter, Junior and his best mate, Jim, and the Mizuki orphans, Barry and Sam.

Sasha, June and Fred were set against Junior volunteering. Fred went as far a speaking to Mike.

"Junior is important to me in helping with my calculations."

Mike agreed but said, "I think you need another assistant, no we can afford to give you two assistants and from other clans. Teach them all you know, that way if something happens to you, all your work will not be lost. After all, you are not getting any younger."

Fred was mortified, "I am not old, I feel fine."

"Indeed," Mike observed, "and have you noticed over the last few years in winter, not so many people have died."

Fred agreed and said, "Because of horses, accidents among the hunters are less."

Mike pondered and said, "I never thought of that and you are right."

Mike chose Fred's two assistants, chosen not at random, he selected Luke and Ben. He had noticed on several occasions that the two were pals, bright, confident and able to stand up for themselves; a trait that had gotten them into trouble quite a few times.

The boys were summoned, excused all duties and were to report to Fred every morning.

The next day, Luke and Ben reported to Fred's hut. "You're late, what time is this?"

Luke said, "You never said when to come." Fred had no answer to that, nevertheless, the three of them walked up to Fred's wall and their lessons began.

* * * *

The expedition members were selected.

Leader Jock, clan's Junior, Jim, Barry, Sam, Barny, Terry and Beks and from the Mizuki, Jude and Buddy.

Three weeks after the midsummer festival, the expedition was ready to leave, head south and meet whatever fate awaited them. Each rider had a packhorse in tow, and as they had no knowledge of the southern clans, where they lived, the land where they lived, how many there was of them, planning was difficult. These southern people did not appear to have horses. Mike impressed on them that they should never find out or see the horses.

"When you find out where they live, keep your distance, move back north a distance well away, set up camp and scout ahead on foot."

John was talking to Fred and Junior, and said, "Remember this, twice we have been attacked by them, they took prisoners and killed everyone else."

Fred said to Junior, "We think we killed them all and none made it back. You are going there to spy and come back, and let us know what you have found out. But if you are discovered, Mike, John and I agree, if possible, you must kill even if you're seen by just two people.

Don't let them escape to warn the rest, you have to kill them."

* * * *

Therefore, in early July, ten men and twenty horses set out on a journey that would take them they knew not where. The people were still living at their summer camp on the plain and everyone, man, woman and child turned out to see them off, but it was a subdued send-off.

Part Four

Chapter Twenty-Two
Geyin – The City of the Adnin

In the southern city of Geyin lived almost two-thousand souls including slaves, ruled by Rufus, priest/king of the Adnin. He had used the technology of the educated political elite and that of their conquered people to expand Geyin. They had farms, an aqueduct, they worked with metal, their stone structures dedicated to the gods, most of whom he had invented in his so-called visions.

In the last two years, a drought had caused the harvests to fail. Rufus came up with a great idea. He got rid of some political opponents by offering them up as sacrifices to appease the gods.

Sacrifices to the gods became the norm with the added bonus of removing his enemies. He ruled by fear and his position was absolute. When opponents ran out, he turned to the slaves. Their unhappy life, made short by overwork, not enough food. Beatings and finally taken for sacrifice.

The soldiers and priests roamed further and further south in search of conquests and slaves with diminishing returns. Rufus needed a victory before his opponents gathered their strength again.

The forest people to the west were a known factor. They had defeated him repeatedly. The two expeditions to the north hadn't returned but why was unknown. He decided not to send small expeditions north as before but an army.

A few weeks later in May, an army comprising of two-hundred soldiers and fifty priests and a hundred slaves carrying supplies set out north.

Only after their departure, did Rufus realise that if this military expedition failed to return like the two previous expeditions, militarily and politically, he would be vulnerable.

Day after day, week after week, the long slow column of men headed north. At nights, some slaves managed to cut their bindings and escape.

The plain's animals gave them a wide berth, food was becoming short, soldiers used to eating from farms and by slaves were poor hunter-gatherers.

By early July, discipline was beginning to break down, the priests who ruled by fear were beginning to lose control. Everyone was hungry. The army didn't know it, they were not even half way to the home of the clans.

As the increasingly shambolic army moved north, Jock was moving south at more than three times their speed. In the vast plain, they would have missed each other, if not, in front of the horsemen rose a tor the like of which no one had ever seen, it was many times the height of the trees on the escarpment. Higher at the south end, lower in the north. At its base it was as wide as any river that the clan had ever seen.

Midday was approaching, the men had not stopped to rest and water their horses. With their needs tended to, everyone went exploring the tor. The northern end was a mass of huge granite boulders, climbing between them was easy. It was noted that overhangs and shallow caves would make for good shelter, and at the lower end, there were blind draws for horses.

Climbing higher, they reached the summit at the northern end. In front of them was a narrow ridge running up to the southern end. In places, it was less wide than a man was tall. At this height, the wind was strong but they had come this far, nothing was going to stop them getting to the summit.

The traverse to the top was slow, in the narrower parts progress was made on hands and knees to stop the wind blowing them of the edge. As they went higher, the going was easier, and at the summit, the view of the great plain was spectacular, they could look south seemingly forever.

Junior looking to the east, spotted a large column of men moving north, and raised the alarm and was joined by everyone. The riders didn't have a word for army but as they watched, it became obvious that this army, and that was all it could be, was moving very slowly.

Barry observed, "At that rate, they will not reach us by midwinter."

No one argued with him.

Jock said, "We can't go on now, we must warn everyone."

Sam said, "Wait a bit before we go back, let's observe them first."

Junior agreed, "Let's find a tor closer."

Jock changed his mind and agreed. The men descended the great tor as fast as they could, and set off north and slightly west to avoid detection.

Less than half a day later, two tors looked a likely spot. The westerly tor would keep the horses hobbled and out of sight, while the Easterly tor was much closer to the advancing column and offered a better view.

Everyone climbed into the rocks of the tor and settled down to wait.

In the distance, the great tor came into view.

"You know," said Barny scratching his chin. "From here, the tor looks like a huge man lying on his back, see his head is higher pointing south, his feet are lower facing us."

No one else could see the likeness but from that day on, the great tor was known as the sleeping man, and eventually when it became a marker on the journeys, both north and south on the great plain, it became known as the Sleeping Hunter.

It was a long wait, it was the next day at midday before the Adnin, gradually, came into view. It would pass in Junior's estimation more than ten tens of paces in front of them. He passed on this estimate to his mates but to himself, he used a word that only he and his dad used that was their word for hundreds.

The column slowly passed Jock and his men. One thing become immediately obvious, this was no army striding out to conquer new lands and people, this was an army in the last stages of hunger and exhaustion.

The priests had resorted to whips moving up and down the column, keeping the shambolic army moving.

"We've seen enough, let's get back home," whispered Jock.

They retreated to their horses and headed north to warn the people of the threat. Before evening, the riders came across a vast herd of aurochs slowly heading north, grazing as they went. The herd was so big, it filled the horizon from west to east.

The hunter in Jock came to the fore.

"You know, if we get ahead of them and spread out, light a few fires and charge them into a stampede, they would stampede right into that army."

The plan was simple and made sense. They rode out in a wide arc to get ahead of the animals, slowing them down to allow time to the slower army to get near.

After a day of riding from horizon to horizon, close enough to the aurochs to make them wary, Junior came back and informed Jock that the army were closer and the next morning would be a good time to stampede the animals.

Fires were prepared and lit, and spread out over many tens of tens and tens of spaces. The riders turning south moved forward, and with shouting, screaming, stopped a huge part of the herd and with a final charge, turned them and drove towards the Adnin army. With part of the herd turned and running south, the rest followed, bearing down on the Adnin.

Chapter Twenty-Three
An Army Slaughtered

The Adnin had never seen anything like it, in front of them as far as the eye could see was a huge black line of animals moving towards them. The dust they kicked up filled the blue sky.

Most of the army stood transfixed as the stampeding animals bore down on them. A few tried to run but there was nowhere for them to run to.

The first of the herd hit the head of the column and carried on with no slacking of pace. If anything, the cries, screams and the smell of blood frightened the animals even further. The leading animals striking the head of the column veered to left and right to avoid the men. The following animals had no option but to plunge further into the column.

Hours later when the herd had passed, Jock was going to ride through the scene of carnage when Junior reminded him.

"Remember, they don't use horses, don't let the survivors see them, some of them may make it back to where they came from."

Barry and Sam, the orphaned Mizuki were in favour of killing all the injured, and said as much, Jock disagreed.

"We'll take a few of the least injured as prisoners but the rest of the living are on their own."

Slowly, the northerners advanced, and with trepidation and with spears at the ready, moved among the Adnin. They needn't have worried about the survivors. The few uninjured and injured alike already in a weak and demoralised state could offer no resistance.

The carnage and injuries were terrible to behold, the screaming and crying of men was almost too much for the men of the clan as they slowly moved among the injured and dying. Despite the language barrier, men pleaded to be put out of their pain. But how could a peaceable man of the clans or a man of the Vornay when confronted with a soldier lying on the ground with a chest or abdomen caved in, bring himself to plunge a spear into his throat to end his pain, but they had to do it, the need of the dying was too great.

They did it over and over, they would never be the same again, memories of that day would haunt them forever.

The sound of the dying and injured eventually quietened down, and at Jock's orders, six of the least injured brought away from that terrible place. Later it turned out that three of the prisoners were soldiers, one was a priest and two were slaves.

The dejected prisoners fed, watered and bound with leather thongs sat on the ground while their captors debated their fate.

Junior, in the few hours that they had been prisoners, had been observing them individually, addressing everyone he asked, "What have you noticed about our prisoners?"

Barry observed, "Do you mean that one man with a shiny plate on his chest."

"Yes, but more than that, the one with a plate on his chest stares us in the eye, we need to be careful of him, I think he could be dangerous."

No one argued. Becks said, "Three of them have leather jerkins but the other two are barely clothed."

Barry noted, "Look at what the two men are wearing. I don't recognise what that is, it's not leather."

Becks agreed, "The three with the leather jerkins are wearing something else under their jerkins. It looks like the same material that the two men are wearing."

Barney said, "If the one with the shiny plate is the leader, why are the rest dressed so differently?"

Junior said, "The shiny one can't be the leader. Among the dead there were more with shiny plates, they can't all be leaders."

Junior said, "These questions will have to wait until we get home, but first we need to search the dead for something." They later found out metal, specially the cutting rods.

And so, before they left that terrible scene, some of the metal and some of the strange clothing was collected and piled together except for a few knives, which were far better than their own flint and bone knives.

Jock said, "When we get home, we will have to come back and collect everything."

The following morning, it rained. It was continuous and heavy, the journey north and home had a miserable start. The prisoners now tethered to the packhorses and soon overcame their fear of the animals. At midday, the rain had eased, and the party stopped in the lee of a stand of trees to eat and drink. It wasn't much, dried meat and water.

Barry suddenly exclaimed, "Did you see that? Shiny plate took the meat from one of the near naked men and he allowed it, he just kept his head lowered."

Sam, the other orphan of the Mizuki, walked up to shiny plate and signalled him to stand up and then promptly knocked him back down. The look of hatred in shiny plate's eyes was evident to all.

Jock observed, "Junior, you are right, we will need to watch that one."

That evening when the beef jerky was being given out, Barry said to Jock, "Let me distribute the meat."

"Why?"

Barry said, "Trust me."

He dished out the beef and water sacks. He went to shiny plate last and standing in front of the sitting priest, he held the last of the jerky and water. Shiny plate held out a hand to receive his portion. Barry turned on his heel and went to the slave deprived of his midday meal, signalled to him to stand up and when he did, Barry gave him the priest's jerky. Spontaneously, the northerners burst into applause and laughter. Even the three captive soldiers didn't look too unhappy, the two slaves after years of intimidation, didn't react at all.

Chapter Twenty-Four
The Expedition Returns

The slow trek north continued hampered by the slaves. They were obviously weaker than the other four. Eventually, Jock called a halt and Barny and Jim moved the packs from two of the animals while Jude and Buddy of the Vornay introduced the slaves to the joys of horse riding. Before they all set off, shiny plate tried to move towards the slaves on horseback but it took one look from Sam to change his mind.

The journey continued day after day. Sometimes, it rained. Sometimes, it didn't. There were no paths on the great plain. There was plenty of boggy ground, streams and rivers. Endless backtracking to find firmer ground or a place to cross was tedious but a mental map of the great plain was forming in the minds of the men, something that would stand them in good stead in the future.

Jock said to Junior, "You know that wall of yours, would it be possible to draw the great plain, and mark the rivers and bogs."

"Yes, it would take time. I could use the tors especially the great tor as a marker, let me think about it."

If it wasn't for the horses, it would have been a nightmare. As they rode, Junior took to riding beside the slaves and tried to talk to them. Progress was slow but after names of things from people to horses, he began to make progress. Noah and Charlie, the slaves became less afraid and more confident. Gradually, the relationship between the slaves, the soldiers and the priest/warrior was revealed.

"How can one man be less than another?" Becks said. "I like some people, some I don't like, but we are all people of the clans."

Junior agreed, "But are we less than Mike or is he better than us. Willy is the best hunter. Does that make the other hunters less than him? I don't know the answer but what I do know is that it's wrong the way Noah and Charlie were being treated."

At last, the plain and the tors started to look familiar, and in the far west, clouds hung over the escarpment. They were nearly home. By mid-afternoon, everyone in the summer camp had seen them. Mike, Fred and Jude's father, Buster, rode out to meet them and before they reached the camp proper, everyone busy or idle came out to meet them and gawp at the prisoners. By this time, shiny plate was no longer shiny plate. His breastplate now removed and added to the others taken from the dead priests. However, he remained aloof and not intimidated by his circumstances.

Jock and his men had a story to tell. Mike and a few others heard of their adventure first, but in the clans' tradition of preserving history by storytelling, the next day, clan and Vornay alike gathered to hear directly of the journey and the capture of the prisoners.

The arrival of Jock and his party, and their prisoners was the biggest thing that had happened to the clans since the arrival of the Vornay. Everyone couldn't wait to hear of Jock and his men's adventures. As evening approached, everyone gathered outside the meeting hut, adults settling down on the ground and trying to make themselves comfortable, children running all over chasing each other, laughing and shouting.

Mike inside the meeting hut smiled.

Fred said, "Why the smile?"

"Do you hear that noise of the people talking, children shouting and screaming, everyone is happy and that's the way it should be."

The hubbub continued, the atmosphere was electric, the sun disappeared behind the high escarpment casting long shadows but there was still plenty of light before the sun would disappear for the night.

Mike and the other clans' leaders led Jock and his team out of the hut, the hubbub lessened, the children quietened down. Jock was nervous and a bit overwhelmed by the huge audience gathered to listen to the adventure, but with the help of Junior who was much more confident, soon found his stride and kept everyone enthralled.

He told them of sighting a huge column of men slowly moving north, how they hid in a tor and watched the approaching column and saw that many of the men in the column were in the final stages of exhaustion. However, there was no doubt in all their minds that these were the monsters that had destroyed the Mizuki clan and the Vornay Fox family.

Then he explained how they decided to head home to warn the people, and how they rode north, they came across a great herd of aurochs, and then rode further north to overtake them and stampede them south into the bad men. He and Junior painted a graphic picture of the aftermath of the herd's passing.

People at this place and this time unused to the written word or pictured scene had a highly developed imagination, and in their mind's eye, everyone listening could picture the scenes as if they were there.

The priest was brought before them, no one needed to be told twice. Jock said, "This man is dangerous, look at the way he holds himself and tries to stare you down. Barry, you tell them of the stolen meat. No!!! Before you do that, Junior, you tell them of priest, soldiers and slaves."

While Barry and Sam led the priest away, Junior stood up.

"I mostly talked to Noah and Charlie, and what I have found is they are of a different clan from the Adnin. Do you remember the terrible things that happened to the Barry and Sam's clan?"

The older members of the clan cried out at the painful remembering, even the younger people knew the story intimately. "And do you remember how we chased after them and their prisoners?" His spellbound audience remembered well and cried out at the memory. "Well, that's what happened to Noah and Charlie's clan," Junior continued. "The Adnin, that's what Noah and Charlie call them, take people from other clans and take them to their city. They keep them prisoner at night, and during the day, they have to work for them. They are called slaves and are beaten if they don't work hard enough and sometimes the priests will kill a slave in a special place, I am not sure why."

The audience were mesmerised, enthralled and angered all at the same time.

Fred's son continued with the story, "The Adnin don't live in caves, some live in wooden huts like us but others like that priest and their chiefs live in stone huts, bigger than the biggest hut we have. The slaves cut and shape stone to make these stone huts."

Tam the flint knapper stood up, "You can't cut stone, it's too hard."

"That's what I said to Noah. He said the stones they use are not like the rocks on the tors on our plain. These rocks are very hard. The rocks the slaves use are not as hard but even then, it can take many days to shape one stone and it takes many shaped stones to make a stone hut. Every night, the slaves are put into big huts, the entrances barred and during the day, they work for the Adnin in the town and in the fields. They build more stone huts. They make weapons of a shiny stuff."

Jock held up a breast plate, the assembled gasped, their imagination was on fire. This was one of the most exciting day everyone had experienced, people cried out, "Tell us more about stone huts."

Others wanted to know, "What was a soldier, what was a priest? What do the slaves do? What are fields?"

Everyone was getting too excited. Mike stood up and called for quiet, and as the strong leader, that was quickly obeyed. "Before this night is over, you will have been told everything but first I like Barry's story on how he dealt with the priest, tell them, Barry."

He stood up and faced the crowd, "The one known as the priest is in charge."

"Like Mike," someone shouted.

"No, no, no, not like Mike. Priests are bad, if you don't do what a priest says, he can have you killed. Anyway, when we gave food to the prisoners, the priest went up to a slave and took the food for himself. The slave was too frightened to do anything about it so when we next fed them, I held out the food to the priest and when he reached out to get it, I snatched it away and gave it to the slave and the priest got nothing."

The already excited audience shouted and cheered.

The evening was growing late, Mike called it a day, "When Noah and Charlie, and possibly the three soldiers, are able to speak better to us, we will meet again

164

and learn more of slaves, soldiers, priests, stone houses, fields and shiny plates."

The days passed, Noah and Charlie no longer considered a threat. They started to put on weight, and were becoming fluent in the language of the clan and when dressed in the clothes of the clan, indistinguishable from the clan, and allowed to roam free.

Barry and Sam allowed them to sleep in their summer tent.

The priest was tied up at all times, and occasionally allowed to walk about the camp, always escorted by two men of the clan.

The three Adnin soldiers seemed not to be a threat and appeared happy with their situation. Tied up at night, and free to wander during the day, often Fred accompanied them.

Fred, Junior, Barry and Sam were the ones who worked more closely with the five Adnin, and as communications and common language improved, the lives and skills of the Adnin became apparent.

The metal knives were a sensation. Mike immediately organised an expedition with horse and travois to collect all the metal tools. He wanted it back before winter, and so a reluctant Jock and Junior led the recovery team and with that superior memory, Jock guided the team avoiding obstructions and tedious backtracking.

Fred and his son, and Fred's two apprentices were the only people in the clans who had learned to count beyond ten. Fred was keen to know how the Adnin counted in numbers.

Noah, the slave had once been an elder in his clan. The Adnin had attacked his village. Many were killed. The survivors including Noah and his wife were taken.

One day, over a mid-day meal with the slaves and the soldiers, Charlie pointed out, "You don't eat bread nor do you eat plants and roots from the fields."

"Bread, we have no word for that," said Fred.

Charlie replied, "Some of the seed heads from grasses around here can be eaten."

Sam said, "I have pulled the heads if grasses and ate the seeds."

Barry replied, "We all have, they don't taste of much but, it doesn't make you sick."

Charlie went on to say, "I am not sure how it's done but I know they use stones to grind the seeds down to a powder and then the husks are blown away by women using large leaves or pieces of bark, the seed powder is gathered up and water is added."

Fred was intrigued like everyone else; he knew there appeared to be many types of grasses on the great plain, it was only recently as feed for the horses that a use had been found for it.

He said, "What do they do with it?"

Charlie said, "I am not sure but if a mixture is left long enough and then heated, it can be drunk from a bowl and it can take away the hunger for a while, we call it gruel and that's mostly what slaves get."

"What else do they do with these grasses?" enquired Sam.

"Well, if you leave the gruel to dry out, it becomes very thick and is even better at taking away hunger."

The soldier Oliver said, "We eat bread, it is better than what the slaves eat. It can be hard or soft. Oh, what I would not give for a piece of bread dipped into a meat stew."

Fred decided that June should hear all about bread, and he sent Noah and Junior along to fetch her.

When they arrived, Fred said to Charlie, "Fields, that's a new word to us."

The lowly ex-slave was enjoying the attention. "I used to work in the flax fields before I was moved to cutting and shaping stone."

Bread, fields, cutting stone, Fred was becoming confused. "Stop, tell us about flax fields and then tell us about cutting stone."

Charlie said, "You eat roots and tubers that you find in the ground, you find bushes with berries when they are in season. Instead of eating everything, why don't you dig up the whole plant and take it near to where you live. Dig a hole and put the plant in the hole, add plenty of water and usually the plant or bush will regrow, and if you only take some of the plant, it will spread and you can take some more later on."

Fred said, "Okay, I can see that it would be good to have plants to eat all the time, but what about in the winter, all plants die."

Charlie sighed, "No they don't. The grasses die back and the leaves from some trees fall off in winter but you all know they will grow again in the spring. It's just the same with what you put into a field."

"Yes, of course, you're right. It's just that we never thought of it like that."

June asked, "Tell us about bread."

No one was quite sure how to make bread. Noah, the slave, was not involved with its production and had rarely tasted it. Harry the soldier had eaten bread often but was unsure how to make.

Jacob said, "I know once the outer husks are blown away, the powder that remains is gathered and mixed with water."

"Just like gruel?" interjected Charlie

"Yes, but they leave it for a while and then pour it on to very hot stones. That's really all I know."

June said, "Does this bread last?"

"It goes bad after a while but it lasts for several days before you can't eat it."

She was intrigued and was determined to experiment on this new food called bread, and left to find some friends, gossip and start on the long road to make bread.

"What is a flax field?" asked Barry.

Jacob replied, "When you captured us, you took our clothes away, they were made from flax."

Junior had forgotten about their clothes.

"I have seen them somewhere."

"At back of our tent, I know where they are. I'll fetch them."

Fred went off to collect them. He brought back a bundle of dirty smelly objects, but when spread out, they were obviously clothes made from a material completely unknown.

Junior held up a piece to inspect closely, wrinkled his nose at the smell and said, "It is made up of fine sinews, even finer than the ones we use to sew leather."

Charlie replied, "It's not sinew, its threads of flax."

Having worked in the flax fields, he knew how to prepare the plant and how to separate the threads of flax from the rest of the plant.

"You pull the plants up by the roots and spread them out on the ground for weeks on end, and you have to keep turning them over to let wind and sun rot the plant. Then you can separate the flax threads from the rest of the plant."

Junior looked again at the prisoner's former clothes. The potential was obvious, dirty and stained as they were, still more supple than the clans' clothes. He made up his mind to take Charlie and the clothes to the clan leaders at their next meeting to show the potential of this type of grass. So he gathered them up and took them to his mum who reluctantly agreed to wash them.

Days later, the freshly washed clothes were returned to Charlie and so began the clans' introduction to weaving.

Charlie took four reasonably straight sticks of wood each about half the length of a man's arm and with animal sinew, he tied the sticks to form a square.

Junior said, "What now?"

"We tie strands of flax from top to bottom many strands to fill the space. Then we tie a long length of flax to a small stick and pass it through the strands alternatively in front of a strand and behind the next. Once that has been done a few times, the strands can be pushed down to the bottom of the frame and gradually the flax cloth builds up."

Junior thought it would be slow work and said, "Some women can be skilled in making flax cloths."

So under Charlie's guidance, the people of the caves on the escarpment having made the change to the plains, started on the long road to finding flax plants to weaving cloth.

Meanwhile, Fred was bored with all the talk of taking grass and making it into food, and taking other types of grass and making it into clothes. He asked Noah to tell him about living in stone caves.

"They don't live in stone caves, they live in stone huts. We have to cut the stone with flint axes and sort of knife made of the same stuff that the priests sometimes wear, the stone near the Adnin town is quite soft and it isn't too hard to cut a square block, the blocks are taken away and put on top of one another to make a hut. Mostly the blocks are joined together with clay to fill the gaps."

Fred was intrigued.

"How high is a hut?"

"Sometimes a hut can be twice the height of a man. The priests have the biggest. Within a hut there is more than one space, there is a narrow space at the back of the hut which leads to another space."

Fred asked why the priests need two spaces inside a hut.

Noah replied, "Oh, more than two spaces, sometimes three or four all separated by a hanging fur or reed mat so you can't look into the next space."

Charlie went on to tell everyone that there is one hut where Rufus and his close priests live.

"It is many, many times the height of a man."

Charlie's description left little to the imagination, it only reinforced the knowledge that the people of the clans and the people of the Vornay, one day, must come face to face with the people of the Adnin.

Chapter Twenty-Five
The Priest Escapes, Fred Is Attacked

One morning, Sam went to untie the three Adnin soldiers and found only two. They were untied but had chosen to stay where they were. The third soldier, Jacob, had escaped with the priest. Hesitantly, the story came out. The priest had somehow freed himself, then freed the soldiers and expected all four to escape. Oliver and Harry refused to go but Jacob agreed. John, the priest cursed the other two and warned if they alerted the clans, the wrath of the god/king Rufus would fall on them. Cowed by the priest, the two soldiers remained quiet for the rest of the night.

Fred surprised them as they made their way to the corrals. He had been studying the night sky lying on his back on a small rise near the corrals, in the dark. The priest almost tripped over him, he didn't hesitate pulling a fence post. He repeatedly struck Fred until it was obvious he was dead.

The two Adnin had never ridden a horse but they had seen it done many times. They didn't even know how to fit a halter but they were desperate, each man took a horse by the mane and led the compliant beasts out of the sleeping camp. At a safe distance and with a struggle they mounted their horses and holding tight to their mounts' mane, set off south. Their pace was not much faster than walking and was just as tiring. They had a five-hour start but their speed would be no match for their pursuers.

Sam went out to get Junior but before he could, a great cry and shouting went out from near the horse corrals. Sam met Junior and they went to the scene of all the commotion, and on reaching, the horse pens, a group of people stood now silent around a body. Pushing through, Junior screamed his anguish. There on the ground was the body of his father, barely recognisable with his head smashed.

Junior dropped to his knees and sobbed beside his father, and held his dead cold hand. Mike appeared and with help from Sam, they lifted the sobbing son to his feet and walked with him home to break the news to June.

The clans and their friends the Vornay were stunned. Life for these people had always been hard, death from other causes had always been common. There was no room for one man to kill another. Everyone depended on each other to survive, and yet, here was the Adnin. They had wiped out the clan Mizuki. They had murdered a whole Vornay family and now while living in the clans' summer village, they had murdered Fred, one of the most respected and revered clansman.

Where were the priest, John, and the soldier, Jacob? Quickly, the clans discovered that two horses were missing from the corrals.

Mike organised a pursuit almost immediately, five hunters including Jude left on horseback with the minimum of provision. To be followed by a larger party with provisions and spare horses. Mike made it plain the escapees must not reach their home with the knowledge of the existence of the clans and almost just as important, the knowledge of horses.

As the pursuers were mounting up, Mike drew Jude aside.

"It would be better if you didn't bring them back alive."

Jude surprised, didn't say anything. Mike ever the leader could see endless trouble if the two Adnins were brought back as prisoners.

He went on, "If you bring them back what will we do with them? It would be better if they died in the fight when you catch up with them."

Mike looked around to make sure no one could overhear.

Jude again didn't know what to say or do. Mike went on, "We can't keep them as captives forever, they might escape again. Do we tie them up and stand over them forever."

Jude said, "Are you saying when we catch up to them you want us to kill them and bring back their dead bodies?"

"Yes, the alternative is when they are brought back, we kill them ourselves. It would be better if they died fighting you. I don't think we can ask someone to kill unarmed men much as they deserve it."

The pursuers moved out and as they rode, Jude had much to think about. In his heart, he agreed with Mike and this young man showed maturity beyond his years and took responsibility on his own shoulders when he decided to tell his companions that the Adnins should not be brought back as prisoners but should be killed rather than captured. He didn't tell them that it was Mike's idea.

He simply said, "It would be better if they died fighting us than us bringing them back as prisoners to keep them forever and ever."

Jude and his companions rode on and on and before midday, the fugitives sighted, the pursuers urged their horses on and picked up speed. The pursued tried to urge their mounts on but to no avail.

In the end, Jude's concerns were unfounded, within tens of tens of paces, the Adnins turned and faced their enemy. Jude and his team charged at full gallop, the summer sun had had dried out the normally boggy ground. The Adnins had no chance against determined, expert hunters and skilled horsemen, well used to bring down prey on the hoof. On the first charge, the two Adnins were dead. The soldier, Jacob was dead before he hit the ground with a spear bigger than he was in his chest. John, the Priest was not so lucky. The spear had entered his stomach but alive in great pain, he lay on the ground and awaited his fate. It was not long in coming, Jude walked up to the fallen priest, asked and received a spear. He grasped it in both hands and finished the priest off with the spear through his neck.

Jude decided not to bring the bodies back home as he said, "These men don't deserve a burial, leave them to the wolves."

They moved away a few tens of paces from the bodies and waited until the following party arrived and everyone agreed to leave the two Adnins to the animals.

Before the pursers had arrived back at the summer camp on the plain, the clan gathered and buried Fred. In the heat of summer, it was imperative that the dead be buried as soon as possible, something that continues to this day.

Junior, his mum and sister stood at his grave.

Fred who was so well thought of, every man woman and child stood behind them. He was buried in his summer clothes and mercifully covered in his winter furs and as the earth was scooped up and thrown on to the grave. Junior threw a slate covered in chalk marks.

Fred in the last few years had taken to marking the passage of days on a series of slates, each slate representing a lunar month and each slate individually marked so they could be laid out in order, Junior, Luke and Ben were the only ones who could read Fred's markings.

That evening in the meetinghouse, everyone agreed to mount another spying expedition to find out more about the Adnin. As before, the same team was elected to go. Leader Jock, clans Junior Jim, Barry, Sam, Barny, Terry and Beks and from the Mizuki Jude and Buddy.

This time there was another volunteer, the ex-slave Noah. Charlie wanted to go as well but June persuaded Mike to make him stay. She wanted to hear more about bread and flax.

Mike didn't want to let Junior go and said as much. After his father's death, Junior seemed to lose interest in his creation, the wall. It had become a bit of a pilgrimage to people. There always seemed to be visitors watching Luke and Ben as they worked on the wall. The two boys when asked, explained the meaning of the symbols and markings and a few brighter individuals began to understand.

Mike sent for the boys and everyone trooped up the hill to the wall. Junior questioned the boys on all the markings and was satisfied that they understood it. In fact, Fred had taken a step back and left the day to day updating to them.

Both men agreed that Luke and Ben were up to the job and Mike gave his blessing to Junior joining the expedition.

Chapter Twenty-Six
A Second Expedition

Preparations were made, goodbyes to loved ones were said. Isla held Jock in a tight embrace. She didn't tell him that she thought that she might be pregnant.

Late summer, eleven men and twenty-two horses headed south. As before, the secret of horses was important to everyone.

Jock had an initial destination, the Sleeping Hunter. From there, the land could be surveyed for miles, marsh and bog avoided, and in later times, the journey south would be reduced by many days by these initial observations coupled by that wonderful memory of the people at that time.

This time their journey wouldn't be cut short by an Adnin army heading north.

* * * *

Rufus was in no position to send one, in any direction for that matter. He had lost without trace two major expeditions, one to the north another to the forest, along with several smaller scouting missions. He was barely able to maintain his authority over his kingdom. Half his army had left the city and never returned, the other half were demoralised and having difficulty with an increasingly restless citizenship. Worse, the soldiers were not in a position to hunt down escaping slaves as they had done previously. The escapes and lack of re-capture had given the slaves hope. Still beaten and degraded but there had been no human sacrifices for months. Slaves were becoming a precious and scarce commodity. The failed summer rains made matters worse.

The drought was now in its third year with hardly any rain. The sun in a cloudless blue sky had dried the fields out. The crops withered and died; the food stores were rapidly emptying. The population, permanently hungry, the slaves were starving.

Chapter Twenty-Seven
Mia

The city of Geyin contained less than two-thousand souls including slaves. The majority of its citizens were not evil. If they were held accountable for their deeds, it would be to say they allowed an evil hierocracy to take control of their lives. They were about to pay the price of years of this acquiesce and inaction. The city was about to fall.

Mankind is destined to repeat this failure time and time again right up to modern times.

Mia was a slave and like all the slaves, she had become painfully thin. Different from most, she was blonde with blue eyes. She stood as tall as any man and there was something about her appearance and manner and the way she held herself that was off-putting. As a result, she had never been taken by the priests never to be seen again, nor beaten and raped by the soldiery.

Mia's father was a slave. He had gone with the army on their expedition to the north, and his name was Charlie.

It had become increasingly easy for a slave to escape. Locked up in their overnight prisons, it wasn't difficult to force a door. The only thing that stopped mass escapes was their physically weak, beaten and downtrodden condition. So Mia intended to follow her father north to this end. She had accumulated a small pitiful store of food squirreled away in different holes and corners and so on a night of a full summer moon, Mia made her escape.

A lift and a push opened her prison. She made her way to her work place, the threshing shed where she collected her store of food, mostly stale bread and a little dried meat. As an afterthought, she went to the bakery where happenchance rows of freshly baked bread awaited distribution. Mia could hardly believe her luck, she filled a flour sack to the brim and carefully made her way out of the city out into the fields at the eastern edge of the city before turning north in search of her father.

Many miles to the north, Jock and his men were making good progress, the summer drought had dried out much of the great plain making tiresome detours avoidable. The observations from the Sleeping Hunter helped plan a route.

They had been on the move from a new moon to the next new moon. Stored food on the pack animals had run out but there was enough game to meet their needs. Once again horses were more than valuable.

Meanwhile, Mia having exited the city headed north. There was no chase after her. She was on her own and she headed north day after day. Streams provided water but her food ran out. She was not worldly wise to find edible roots and tubers. In the last three days, her only sustenance was a few unripe berries. Her stomach was empty which was a good thing for in the distance she saw activity, birds flying up into the air others landing. In her innocence, she headed towards this activity.

The smell hit her first but she carried on a few tens of paces only to come upon the most awful scene imaginable. Mounds of rotting putrid human bodies not one of which could be recognised as an individual person. If her father was one of these bodies, it would have been impossible to recognise him.

Mia just wanted to get away. She turned east to bypass that terrible place before heading north again.

If Mia had circumvented the scene by turning west, this story may well have had a different outcome. But fate is not just a fickle thing, in the long years of human existence, not all happenings are bad and this time fate smiled on Mia, as she turned east. Jock and his team arriving at the terrible scene had no wish to investigate and they too turned east before continuing south.

Mia was walking and stumbling in a daze, already in a weakened state. She was starving, she had just come across the most awful scene. She walked on hardly aware of her surroundings and didn't see the approaching horsemen. A lone female figure stumbling and obviously in the last stages of exhaustion, she could not and was not a threat. The horsemen quickened their pace towards the girl. As they approached, Noah recognised her.

"This is Charlie's daughter, Mia," he shouted, "MIA, MIA, MIA!"

She stumbled on oblivious to the men and the shouting.

Everyone dismounted, Noah and Jude ran forward. Jude caught her in his arms as she collapsed and laid her down gently on the ground. Noah called for water. After a few sips, she turned her head away.

Jock said, "Look at her, she is starving. It's food she needs."

Jude went to his horse and from a pouch, took out a strip of dried, meat looked at it and realised it was no good for Mia.

He bit a piece off, took some water and chewed until the meat was soft. He knelt beside the semi-conscious girl and holding her head up and with his fingers he transferred a tiny piece to her lips. A few seconds later, Mia's tongue licked the morsel, she swallowed it and started on her road to recovery.

Jock realised there was no point in moving on, so an early camp was set up, horses were attended to. sleeping furs set out, a fire lit for the evening meal. During all this time, Jude never left Mia's side. Every now and again, he transferred softened meat to her lips. Mostly it was ignored and was wiped off, but occasionally, Mia licked her lips and took in the sustenance.

The next day at about midday, Jude had been attending to Mia for nearly twenty-four hours. She was showing signs of recovery and had sipped a little water and when food was pressed to her lips, mostly she swallowed and was gradually becoming aware of her surroundings.

Jock questioned Noah about what he knew about her, "I understand she is Charlie's daughter. What else can you tell us about her?"

Charlie knew her he had seen her many times in different slave jobs.

"What I can say, she always helped a slave if they fell to the ground or was beaten. She would stop and help, this led to beatings on her a few times."

Jock mused, "She must have escaped. She can tell us more about the Adnin and their city than all the spying we can do."

And so after some discussion, camp was set up and everyone waited on the recovery of Mia.

One day later, she was fully conscious, drinking and eating, and talking and listening to Noah, but her eyes never strayed far from Jude who was always there.

The summer evening was drawing to a close. Noah approached Jock and said, "If you want to talk to Mia, she is ready I will translate."

Mia, daughter of Charlie, was an intelligent and observant slave. Before she escaped, she was witnessing and understanding the demise of the city of Geyin and its people, the Adnin.

"The rains have not fallen for many moons, the river that fed us has all but dried up, the fields are barren. The crops have failed, their animals are being slaughtered for food before they died of hunger and thirst. The soldiers no longer control the slaves or the people, many have deserted and gone home to their families, no one seems to care. The priests and their king, Rufus, have retreated to the temple and have not been seen for moons."

Jock wasn't sure what a temple was but let it go, he asked, "How many slaves are there?"

Thinking about the slaves made Mia cry, "There are maybe five tens but they are starving, most can barely walk, they are dying."

Noah translating for Jock said, "Do the Adnin have horses?"

Mia looked confused Noah said, "These animals that you can see with us, I know they didn't have any when I was there. Do they have them now."

Mia said, "No."

Jock was relieved, he asked Mia, "Do the people of the city have any enemies?"

Mia thought and said, "Soldiers have gone to the forest to the west on many occasions and few have returned."

Chapter Twenty-Eight
The Clan and the Tufek

That evening as the sun set, everyone gathered around the fire. Jock spoke, "It seems the Adnin, while still a threat to us, may no longer be a danger if we can find allies in these forest people and join with them. We will not only be able to spy on them, we may be able to defeat them."

He said to Noah, "I never thought to ask how many people live in the city?"

Noah replied, "I don't know, I don't even know if you have the words. All I can say that there are many tens of ten."

Junior said, "Is there more people in Geyin than the number of days from one midsummer to the next midsummer?"

Noah the former slave had a greater understanding of numbers than the clan with the exception of Fred, Junior, Luke and Ben and now only Junior and the boys.

He thought, then said, "I think if you take the number of days from one midsummer to the next and then for the next ten midsummers, that is the number of people including slaves that live in the city."

Everyone was appalled, the number of citizens and slaves was unimaginable.

Mia said, "Many slaves have escaped, some soldiers and citizens too have left and moved south in the hope of finding food."

The news that there were so many people in the city made Jock unhappy, "I was beginning to think we could attack the city instead of spying on it but there are too many people, even if all the clans and the Vornay came south we might not be able to overwhelm so many people."

The next morning as agreed the party headed ever south but angled west in the hope of meeting with another enemy of the Adnin.

The days passed too many for Mia. She felt they were going in the wrong direction; they should be moving north away from the Adnin city.

Mia now rode a horse. Its pack had been redistributed and Jude had helped her in her introduction into horse riding. They often rode together and Jude was teaching Mia the language of the clans with a little bit of his own language mixed in.

In less than two tens of days, the western forest was sighted. The party headed for the forest edge.

"What now?" said Jude.

Jock said, "We keep going south. If we don't go into the forest, maybe the people will see that we mean no harm."

The journey south continued and three days later, they reached the river, the one that flowed through Geyin and now flowed into the forest except what was once a great river many paces across was now reduced to a mere trickle.

Jock decided that this was a good place to stop, and wait and see if the people of the forest would come to them.

They didn't have to wait long, within hours of setting up camp and tending to the horses, a group of natives came out of the trees and stood patiently awaiting events to unfold.

Jock and Noah walked out to meet them and stopped ten paces from them. Jock surveyed these possible allies, they were all men seven in number and smaller than the men of the clan, slightly darker skinned than the clan and obviously not under nourished.

Noah spoke in the language of the Adnin their reaction was instantaneous blowpipes and spears raised. Jock jumped in front of Noah, took four steps forward and raised his hands. Noah changed his words of greeting immediately and assured the natives that they meant no harm and came in peace.

The forest people slowly lowered their weapons. One man took a step forward and spoke to Noah in the language of the Adnin. Much to the frustration of Jock, the conversation was long and drawn out with much waving of arms and pointing. Eventually, Noah turned to Jock and the rest and explained,

"This man, Davy, was a slave, he escaped many moons ago. I told him that I was a slave and was rescued by you, the clans and their allies the Vornay Clan. I told them that you had been attacked by the Adnin and were here on a mission to avenge the deaths of their friends and families."

Chapter Twenty-Nine
Into the Forest

Jock, through Noah, invited the men of the forest to the camp to inspect the horses and have something to eat. It turned out their journey had been watched for some time, and the horses were a source of fascination and they were eager to closely inspect the animals.

A fire was lit in order to prepare and roast meat. Davy spoke to one of his men who promptly left and disappeared into the forest. He returned a short time later with three women carrying woven baskets with various fruits and vegetables.

While they ate, Noah and Davy nattered away in the tongue of the Adnin much to the frustration of everyone else. The talking went on and on, eventually when it was all done, Noah explained their conversation, "I told Davy all about the clan and the Vornay and how you all live in peace, as they do. They call themselves the Tufek. Davy says we should go into the forest and meet with the headmen of the villages. He said there are many escaped slaves in the villages, they can be of help to you."

It was too late in the day to meet the Tufek, Davy promised to come back in the morning and lead them in and meet the headmen of all the villages.

True to his word, Davy came back with ten and ten of the Tufek to escort them to a village.

Barny said, "Can we trust them? Once we are in the forest, we could be trapped."

Jock considered, "I don't think so, Noah, what do you think, ask Mia what she thinks."

The two, much to everyone's frustration, gibbered on in the tongue of the Adnin.

"I don't think that the Tufek will attack us, Mia agrees. We both have worked with Tufek slaves, they are at heart a peaceable people."

And so Jock led a long line of men and horses into the forest.

The Tufek had moved their villages deeper into the forest and it took nearly a day to reach the nearest village. The clan used to forest areas, the Vornay less so and the horses even less.

The horses were spooked by the unfamiliar noises and due to the closeness of the trees, progress was slow.

But eventually they arrived at a clearing. There were a few small huts smaller than the clans'. But dominating the village was one huge hut. It was set off the ground on poles, with steps at each end and in the middle leading to a wide walkway running the entire length of the hut. There were children everywhere along with what appeared to be unbelievable to Jock and his men, small wolves and birds. All of them running about jumping up and down. Jock didn't have a word to describe the scene. Observers in later years would describe the scene as mayhem.

The long column of riders and their escorts moved out of the trees and into the clearing, the birds clucked and proceeded to ignore the intruders. The wolves more cautious and kept their distance. The children and adults ran up the stairs and peered down from the safety of their home.

Hugh, headman of the village, came down from the hut and spoke to Davy and some of the escorts meanwhile all the riders dismounted and stood patiently by their horses. Davy introduced Hugh to Jock and with the help of Noah translating, the pair walked down the line of men and horses stopping to introduce or explain. Jock was anxious to unload the horses and get them fed and watered. Once done and the horses hobbled and guarded by Jude and Mia, who welcomed every opportunity to be alone together.

They all trooped up the stairs to the communal house of the forest people and went in. The space was light and airy with many openings in the walls. Suspended above each were wooden boards held up with rope. It was obvious that the boards could be lowered when the weather turned bad

Barry thought openings in walls a good idea to let in light and wood to shut them an even better idea. He determined to speak to Ash when he got back.

Junior was reminded of his old cave; instead of stone the partitions were of wood.

The Tufek lived communally and they ate communally. The meal at the end of the day was always the highlight of that day and with their guests, tonight was going to be a great occasion. Children ran everywhere. Dogs, for that was their name, lay close by looking for scraps.

The clan had never tasted the meat of a bird and coupled with vegetables and fruit never seen before in all their lives, the clansmen enjoyed the feast as never before.

Jock noticed many of the people were dressed like the people of the city.

Hugh explained, "Escaping slaves wore the clothes of the Adnin but most of the clothes came from the battle by the river."

Through Noah the men of the clans heard about the slaughter of the Adnin in the river.

Hugh, Jock and Noah talked about the Adnin.

Jock said, "Mia says the people are starving."

Hugh called to an ex-slave recently escaped. Noah and the ex-slave talked for seemingly a long time, frustratingly for clan and Tufek alike, when all the talking was done and through further questions to the ex-slave by both clan and Tufek, it appeared that the citizens of Geyin were in no position to defend themselves.

Jock's attitude changed again, now it seemed possible that the city could be overwhelmed. Hugh agreed and volunteered some men. He sent runners to other villages to gather more men, and so that night clan and Vornay went to sleep happier than the day before.

Chapter Thirty
To the City

The next morning, more Tufek arrived and plans for an expedition to Geyin started. Jock appreciated the value of horses and the value of co-operation with his new allies. He suggested that the remaining ten packhorses be given to the Tufek and ten lucky or maybe unlucky men selected for training. Once having mastered the art of mounting and dismounting, the ten were led around the village by ten apprehensive villagers.

The children loved the sight of fellow villagers on horseback. A gaggle of children followed each horse and rider. The ever-patient Vornay horses took it all in their stride and within a short time, the village resembled a carnival.

Jock remembering past summer festivals on the great plain now seemingly so long ago, offered to lift children on to the back of the riders. He was overwhelmed so much so that the rest of his men brought out the rest of the horses and the great parade began.

Some children had the proudest moments of their short lives when they were hoisted onto the back of a horse and held on tight to his or her father and by the end of the day, the ten villagers while not competent, were certainly not incompetent horsemen.

* * * *

The next morning, the expedition departed. In the trees, horses were led by their fellows. But once out on the plain, leading was no longer necessary. All twenty-two horses followed in line accompanied by, in Jock's estimation, ten and ten of Tufek not only armed with their fearsome blowpipes but sharp metal blades recovered from the battle of the river, some of which had been presented to the clan.

It took a day and a night and most of the following day for the riders to see in the distance the city.

Camp without fires was set, double watchers posted throughout the night. They had nothing to report, and as the new day dawned, everyone was up and ready to move.

Jock said, "You all heard what Mia and the other escaped slaves had to say about the state of the city. That was many tens of days ago, things may have got worse. I don't really know but this is what we should do, we ride towards the city, if we are attacked, we can easily out run any opposition and we can protect our new friends if we have to withdraw."

Jude said, "I don't think it's necessary to hide the knowledge of horses."

And so clan, Vornay, two former slaves and ten and ten forest people set off towards the city of Geyin.

* * * *

It was possible that the long drought was ending. As the morning moved on, the sky darkened with black rain clouds and rain threatened. The riders and their accompanying forest people moved slowly towards the city following a well-worn path beside what had once been a great river, now a muddy trickle.

The dry rough ground gradually gave way to a path alongside what were once cultivated fields. The fields were dry and abandoned.

Jock observed, "Is this what Charlie said was fields."

Noah agreed.

In the near distance, the outskirts of the city began. As they slowly approached, the houses were seen to be not much different in shape than what the clan was building on the escarpment. The difference was there were no animal hides as part of the walls and roofs, instead the houses were made from wood, clay and straw. The only noise was the wind swirling between the houses kicking up little dust devils. For the first time in months, clouds obscured the sun.

They rode on, the silence was unnerving; there was no sign of the citizens. Gradually, the construction of the houses changed now partly built with stone blocks as a base. Further on they moved into a large open space with roads leading out on the left and right with a large wide avenue leading up a hill to the biggest building that anyone had ever seen, seemingly made entirely of stone.

The party slowly and warily rode up the wide avenue towards this tremendous structure. As they rode on, the buildings on either side of the avenue got bigger and bigger. They all appeared to be shuttered, and deserted. Finally, they came to a halt on a flagstone-covered area before broad stone steps leading to a platform half way up the building.

Jock with sense of theatre, lined up all twenty-two horses at the foot of the steps. In between each rider stood a Tufek.

"What now?" said Terry in a hushed voice.

He needn't have asked and before anyone could reply, with screaming and shouting, ten and ten of armed priests led by Rufus rushed down the steps. Jock and the rest of the line took a few paces back, allowing them to meet this enemy on level ground. They watched Rufus and the priests run down the steps.

Jude observed, "Look at them, most are old and some are fat."

The fact that most of their enemy were on horses, something none of the Adnin priests and their king had seen before, didn't seem to deter them. Fat and obviously out of breath, Rufus ran at Barry, the orphan from the lost clan Mizuki, who took final revenge on behalf of his clan. His spear jabbed uselessly off Rufus's breastplate but his second jab pierced his throat. Beside him, Sam the other orphan held a bladed weapon in both hands and as Rufus staggered back, blood spurting from his throat, Sam swung the sword with all the strength of a fit young man and decapitated Rufus.

The priests fared no better with their king dead, the fight went out of them but, there was no chance of surrender, as they fell back a few paces their antagonists as one moved forward and without exception cut them all down with barely a scratch on themselves.

The wounded killed.

What followed was a long silence broken only by agitated horse pawing on the flagstone.

Chapter Thirty-One
The Palace

Barny was the first to notice they were being watched. In the distance at the very beginning of the avenue, a crowd of people could be seen standing and staring. Closer to them people could be seen peering round the corners and entrances of the nearer buildings.

Then the first few drops of rain started to fall, lightly at first but soon building up to a deluge. Everywhere people came out on the streets and with upraised arms, welcomed the rain. Moreover, they looked on the demise of their hated king and the breaking of the drought as a good omen brought about by these warriors. Gradually, the citizens of the city despite the pouring rain, in fact welcoming it, moved up the avenue towards what they thought off as their saviours.

The crowd stopped and gaped at the fallen priests and the blood-soaked paving.

Jock said to Noah, "Round up a few and make them move the bodies out of our sight."

Noah grabbed a few men and ordered them to drag the fallen priests out of sight around the corner of the building. They were reluctant to move until Jock, astride his horse, moved right up to them and side swiped a man with his horse's rear. They got the message and the dead were dragged out of sight leaving the rain to wash the blood away.

The rain didn't help the appearance of the people. It was obvious that they were in very poor condition. All were thin and gaunt.

Terry said, "There's too many of them, how can they be fed?"

"It's not our problem," Noah quickly replied.

Jock thought and said, "Yes, it is. We need to help them. Some of the priests were fat they must have a store of food. Terry, Sam go inside and see what you can find."

The two men ran up the steps to the building and hesitated before entering the biggest building they had ever seen.

Mia seeing their hesitation told everyone, "This is the priest king's palace. He and the priests lived there. Many slaves entered and were never seen again and not just slaves, some of his own people were taken as well. This is an evil place."

Jock had a thought.

"Mia, what about the slaves? Do you want to go and see what has happened to them, take Jude."

Mia and Jude mounted up and started to go down the hill when Mia had a thought.

"Jock, these people are in a bad way, the slaves must be worse. Can I take them food?"

Jock said, "Best just take water for now Mia. Jude, remind Mia how we had to attend to her when we first found her." They set off down the hill, skirting the crowd standing quietly in the rain.

Terry came out of the palace and beckoned to Jock, "Come and see this place, all of you come and see."

Jock nodded, he took his men and a few Tufek up the steps leaving the rest of the forest people to guard the palace and entered the grand hall. To a people who until recently had lived in caves, a people who lived in huts in a forest, to a horseman from the eastern plain, the great hall was awesome. No one had the words to describe it properly, it was huge.

* * * *

Opposite the entrance ran a balcony, it reminded Junior of the terrace in the cave by the sea. Except this was higher, wider and had a wall of the smoothest stone he had ever seen, access to balcony was by steps on either side of the hall not rough, hewed steps like the sea cave, these stairs were of the same polished stone as on the balcony. Below the balcony were four entrances and as everyone started to make sense of what they were, seeing polished stone were everywhere blocks of stone on the walls, floor and high up even on the roof. Junior went over to the nearest wall and ran his hand across the stone. It was so smooth that he could feel no bumps cracks or indentations, the join between one block and the next was so close he could barely see the joint.

On the walls and on the stairs were cut holes niches, in them were all manner of things, too many to take in all at once. Junior made a note to come back when he had time to examine them all. What he did see in the little time he had before Jock called him over, was weapons made of the metal. The ones soldiers used, breast plates, headgear all made of metal. In other niches were stone carvings of delicate flowers, carved heads, jars bigger than anything the clan had and were beautifully decorated. Far too good for everyday use.

The more they looked the more they saw. Set in the walls were metal frames holding candles, not the poor wicks made from animal hair and set in a pool of animal fat that the clans used but somehow the fat was solid and shaped. There were as Jock observed, "Many tens of tens of these holders."

Each holder usually had five candles, only Junior could count the total.

Attention now turned to the four entrances below the balcony. As everyone approached, they could see that each entrance led to steps leading down into complete darkness.

Jock turned to Becks, "Can the holders on the wall be removed?"

Becks went to the nearest holder and easily removed it from the wall. Barry went to his horn and gently blew on it and soon produced a flame to light the candles. Jock took the candles and approached the left entrance. The flickering light showed that the steps went straight down, gingerly, Jock took a few steps down.

Becks appeared behind him, with another holder, everyone plucked a holder and lit the candles and followed the two men down the stairs.

The stairs turned in on themselves but continued downwards and after many tens of tens of steps, they came out onto a large hall, the light of the candles was insufficient to light the whole area but there were other holders on the walls, when their candles were lit, the entire area was lit.

Opposite the stairs about ten and ten and ten paces from them were rows of wooden panels higher than the height of a man. They appeared held in place by wooden spars set horizontally across, keeping the panels in place. Jock nodded to Barny who went to the extreme left panel and removed the spar. Instead of the panel falling down, it swung open, the clan had come across their first door.

There was no time however to examine this new construct. Jock and Becks holding their candles went into the entrance and immediately recoiled in horror and backed out of the room, it was full of dead bodies.

Not just corpses, these bodies had been there for a long time. The smell of death was long gone although it was obvious that the rats had not left the dead alone.

Before looking in the other doors, Jock beckoned everyone to look in at the corruption.

Jock said, "The men we killed, priest, soldiers, they must have been responsible for all of this."

Sam said, "How did they die?"

Junior went back to the door.

"I think they died of hunger."

There were three doors left, no one wanted to find what was behind them. Jock himself removed the bars and found like the first room it was more of the same except that the dead were more recent and opening the last door, the smell of corruption was overpowering and just before Jock shut and barred the door, he saw mounds of bodies seemingly almost alive and moving until he realised it was the rats gnawing and crawling over the dead that gave the impression of movement. Barring the door, he didn't allow anyone else to look in, simply saying, "More of the same except worse." No one argued.

In silence, everyone retreated up the stairs. With three more sets of stairs, surely there could be no more dead.

The next set of stairs was exactly the same as the first with a large chamber at the bottom, this time there were no doors leading off instead piled everywhere were bundles of dried meat, mounds of what was later discovered to be grain, piles of rotting vegetables as well as a large pool of water. There were four slaves each armed with a long stick. As they approached, they retreated into the furthest corner and like the slaves that they were, stood with their heads down.

Noah advanced and spoke to them. He turned and said, "These slaves are kept here to stop the rats from eating the food."

Jock said to Noah, "Go back outside and explain to the people about this food and bring some of them down to carry the food out."

"I don't think they will come, everyone is frightened of this place."

In the event, Jock sent Becks, Jim and Buddy outside with Noah, shortly after they returned shepherding four reluctant citizens. Jock explained to Noah that the citizens should go and collect their eating bowls and if they wanted to eat, return and wait outside.

"Take these men and tell them to spread the word."

Noah left with the four citizens, he returned shortly leading Jude and Mia to the rest of the team, then left to organise the transport and distribution of food to his former masters. Surprisingly, he bore no ill will to them and was enjoying his newfound status.

* * * *

Mia made straight to Jock, "The slaves are in worse condition than the people standing outside, most can barely walk."

"How many are there?" asked Jock

"About five tens of tens, but I think some of them will die."

Jock said, "Let's see what we can do, Junior can you take Barry and Sam and see what's at the bottom of the other two stairs? Hopefully there will be no more dead people."

And with that everyone went back up to the grand entrance. Junior, Barry and Sam left to investigate further while everyone else stepped out on to the top of the entrance steps and enjoyed the fresh air after the fetid and gruesome atmosphere downstairs.

Beck, Jim, Buddy and Noah stood in line at the top of the steps looking down on a few hundred citizens of Geyin, all of them holding bowls or plates.

"My word," said Junior. "News travels fast in this place."

Mia said, "We should feed the slaves first but how?"

Noah came up with the answer. At the top of his voice he shouted to the citizens. "The slaves will be fed and watered first, not one of you will be fed until they have."

Jock went down the stairs and started pushing wet, reluctant, frightened citizens up the stairs where they were directed down to the food store emerging with food in their bowls and carrying skins of water, but instead of distributing the food to the waiting crowd, Jude and Mia led them down the hill towards the building that housed the slaves.

Jock suddenly ran down the hill and shouted to them to stop. When he caught up, he advised them to give the food sparingly.

"In the caves, I have seen hungry people. When they suddenly get food, they eat too much and make themselves sick. Wait here and I will send Terry down to give you a hand."

By the time he got back up the hill, there was a slow line of citizens with empty platters going up the steps and a slightly faster line going down the steps with food in their bowls, and instructed to return tomorrow.

Junior thought about the unexplored part of the building. He and Jock went up the staircases, Junior on the right Jock on the left. At the top they both turned to the banister and looked down.

"This is where Rufus would command his people. I can just see him shouting out his orders to his priests. I have seen something like this before. When I was a boy, we found a cave by the sea. It had a terrace a bit like this, though not as grand. It had been abandoned. We thought that the leader of those people whoever they were would stand like this and speak to his people."

"A bit like Mike at the meeting tent."

"Yes, but at least we can speak to Mike."

The two men turned and examined the entrance opposite the balcony, it was taller and wider than the entrances underneath the balcony.

"I don't think we'll find any bodies through there."

Junior agreed, "This will be where Rufus and his priests lived."

Their observations proved correct. They were confronted by a corridor, which in Jock's estimation had ten and ten of what they later came to understand were doors. Junior more accurately counted twenty-one.

Behind some doors were slave women. Junior corrected Jock's observations, "Some are just girls, not full-grown women."

Jock paused, "You are right."

The girls were in five of the rooms and numbered more than ten. They cowered against the far wall when the two clansmen entered. The men turned and left, unwilling to distress them more than they already were, but as they left the rooms, Jock took notice of the walls. They were covered with brightly coloured hangings depicting all sorts of animals and images of men hunting the animals, and as they turned to leave one of the rooms, Junior observed, "Those benches with furs and coverings must be where they sleep, not like us lying on a bed of leaves and moss."

Their exploring continued, other rooms proved to be storage for weapons, others for storing clothes. In their home caves, storage of goods were on suitable stone shelves sometimes artificially enlarged. In their new homes on the escarpment some rough shelves were constructed, but nothing like the wooden shelves storing clothes. The shelves were arranged round three walls and ranked one above another almost to the ceiling. In the middle of the room was a large flat wooden board supported by poles at each corner.

Another room proved to be their eating area with benches and another massive platform supported by upright wooden poles.

"We could use that idea at home," said Jock. "I am always spilling food on to my lap."

Junior walked to the far end of the room and discovered a small room with shelves holding rows and rows of pottery. "You know," said Junior, "these people were very clever. What went wrong? Why were they so cruel?"

"Maybe they weren't all bad, maybe it was just Rufus and his priests. When you look at the crowd outside, they didn't look like the murderers that we met before/" Jock agreed.

The two men continued on their exploration, at one end, they found a room with holes on the floor,

Jock laughed, "They didn't need to go outside for a pee."

At the back of the room was a pit set in the floor big enough to hold four men at once. Later they learned that slaves would fill it with hot water and the priests used the pit to wash.

The last two rooms were for food preparation and cooking and further storage of food. Both men agreed that how could some people live so well but allow so many others to suffer and starve.

Some of the slave girls under the guidance of Noah were taken down to the slave quarters, all of them carrying food from Rufus's upper food store. Before setting off Noah, Jock and Junior took them to look at the bodies of their former masters. The girls just stood and stared. Junior thought that it would be a long time before they would be able to forget their time with the priests.

Before Jock and his team left on their quest, they had seen the beginning of flax cultivation, a precursor of weaving.

Junior was minded of the storeroom of clothes. And so in a lull in events, everyone including most of the Tufek trooped up to the clothing stores. After a good rummage around, some laughter, posing and strutting, which relieved the tension of that first day, everyone was suitably attired in the softer and more comfortable linen clothes of the Adnin.

Jock was discovering that the mantle of leadership had its downside. He suddenly realised that he was responsible for the well-being not only of the clan but the Tufek warriors.

Food was not immediately a problem. But where was everyone to sleep tonight, who would stand guard over men and horses. He did what all good leaders did, he delegated.

"This is what we should do. Sam and Jim, take forest warriors and prepare the evening meal."

He continued, "Junior, Noah and Davy, can you work on a rota in which men took a share of guarding their fellows."

Noah and Davy strolled down the hill to the first of the big stone huts and with little trouble evicted the owners, more huts followed. Noah estimated that everyone could be accommodated in four of the big huts. Noah took some pleasure in evicting some of the more elite citizens of the city.

Everyone else was heading to the priests' eating place when Terry arrived informing them that Jude and Mia were staying with the slaves for the night and were asking for more assistance in the morning.

He asked for water, food and firewood and said, "And some of the fine clothes I see you have found."

Becks said, "Come on, I will show you around."

And he took Terry on a tour of the upper floor.

Later in the eating room, clan and Tufek sat self-consciously on benches at what they later found out was called a table. The rest sat on the benches around the walls or on the floor and talked about the day and what to do tomorrow.

Junior was eager to go home and was all for leaving the Adnin and their city of Geyin to their own devices.

Jock was not so sure.

"Today, in this place, we cut off an evil head. If we leave, another might grow."

"So," said Buddy, "what do we do?"

Jock was quiet for a moment.

"Before we leave, we need to get the city working again, it appears their drought is over. Noah, you know this place better than anyone here, what should we do?"

Buddy said, "Noah is a slave, why should he help them?"

Noah stood up.

"I was a slave, not now. For that I thank you. My people are long gone, the few that are left are recovering in the slave quarters, I've nowhere to go. The people of this city are not all bad, most have suffered like the slaves although not as bad. I will help if I can."

Junior enquired, "What do you suggest?"

It was Noah's turn to be quiet for a moment.

"In the morning, people will come looking to be fed. More than that, they are coming to us, looking for us to feed them. While we have them all here, let's get the farmers, the weavers, the bakers, the cutters of wood, all the people who can get the city working. If we can do that, you can go home."

He was quiet again for a few moments.

"Food is short. It will be sometime before the Adnin can feed themselves," he said to Davy. "You can use things this city can provide; you supply food and fuel the city can provide things for your villages especially the platters and bowls." He stopped and turned, "That you can see being brought in by our friends."

With perfect timing, the food arrived.

The eating room was crowded and was becoming noisily good-humoured. There is nothing like sharing food to make friends.

Davy agreed that food could be available in exchange for goods that were within the city, and said, "Even if the headmen agree, it will be difficult to send food to the city."

"Travois," said Jock, "we can make them for you."

What followed was a discussion on the distribution of horses and men and the construction of the travois. Junior had an idea. If food is coming from the Tufek, why can't the horses drag two travois one behind the other.

Jock snapped his fingers, "Great idea." Then added, "We are hunters, let's find what animals roam in this place."

In the end, ten horses would be clan's and two kept as pack animals for the return journey. That left ten of the original ten of which two were for the use of Noah and Davy.

It had been a long day; Junior could hardly believe it had only been one day, so much had happened. It was dark when Noah took them to their new sleeping houses further down the hill.

This was their first day in the city of Geyin.

The Second Day

The next morning, Davy left with proposals for the villages. With him went one of his men and Barny, Terry and Becks and ten horses loaded with goods, clothes, cooking and eating utensils, some made of metal, weapons and anything else that took Davy's fancy.

Jock said to his fellow clansmen, "If the Tufek agree to send food, start building travois as many as you can; Junior's idea of each horse dragging two travois is a good idea."

Barry, Sam and Jim rode out south to see if there were any herd animals that they could hunt and possibly herds of wild horses. They returned late in the afternoon with nothing to report.

That same morning as predicted, the people turned up to be fed. Instead, Noah kept them waiting. They had barely started to arrive when the rain came on again, no one complained.

Noah, a former headman himself was proving to be a good administrator. Before anyone ate, they were pushed and shoved into the various guilds; farmers, bakers and their assistants, metalworkers and assistants, stonemasons, labourers.

The former slave and soon to be leader of the city of the Adnin commanded that every guild and group of citizens by the next morning present a leader of his guild to him.

Further, have plans now that the drought appeared to be over, to start the city running again, only then did he allow them food.

They were to understand that the store of food would not last much longer and there would be hungry times ahead.

The rest of the day was for exploring the city. The men of the clan wandered about at will looking into houses great and small and soon came to the conclusion that only a few lived in a grand style. Some of the Adnins' living conditions were worse than that of the clans in their new village on the escarpment.

Jock and Junior wandered about, then decided to go down to see how Jude and Mia were getting on. As they wandered down the hill, they spied groups of men standing together in several groups with much talking and waving of arms. He didn't like what he saw. They went back and collected Noah and their horses and went back and rode slowly into and among the citizens.

Noah talked and listened, then riding up to the two men laughed.

"It's not what you thought. They're not planning to attack us, they were doing as we ordered. Organising themselves into groups and electing a leader."

Relieved, Jock said, "Show us where the slaves are."

The three men rode to the very last of the houses. As they rode, they looked out onto rain-soaked bare ground where the crops once grew to feed the city. Already a few men were planting seeds in the vain hope of a harvest before winter set in.

The three turned right between the fields and increasingly decrepit hovels, riding on until they reached four large buildings. Noah explained, "The two buildings beside the field are where slaves are kept at night, that was where I used to live. The other buildings are where the soldiers lived who guarded the slaves."

Jock and Junior armed with captured metal weapons drawn rode slowly and carefully towards the soldiers' buildings but just then Jude appeared.

"There's no one there, they've all run away, mostly to their families in the city."

All three riders swung round and headed to the slave houses.

Dismounting and tying their mounts, they entered the house of slaves. Junior wrinkled his nose at the smell.

Jude said, "You should have seen this place when we first came, there were dead and dying everywhere. It's bad but not as bad as yesterday, we moved the dead around the back of the house but, there are too many for us to bury."

Mia escorted Jock round, "How many are there?"

Mia cried and wept, "I don't know."

Jock turned to Noah, "Bring down as many citizens as you can. Find especially the people from the big houses where we slept last night. I want the slaves that can be helped taken to the city proper and the dead buried as soon as possible, and when they're finished, I want the dead from the king's palace removed and buried. If it's not all done today, none of them eat tomorrow until it is done."

Within the hour, clan and Tufek warriors escorted many tens of Adnin to the house of slaves. The people appeared to be shocked at what they found and saw. Junior remarked, "I don't think many of them knew what was going on."

The gruesome task of burying began, meanwhile Mia and Jude organised the move of the living to the city proper. Some could walk with assistance, others carried on wooden platforms taken from the soldier's house.

Jock and Junior watched the pitiful procession, slowly making their way to the city. They rode on ahead to make sure there was places for them all when they arrived.

This was only their second day in the city.

Third Day

The morning of their third day started as usual with crowds forming outside the great house of Rufus, waiting for food.

No one was going to eat until the great house was cleared. There was so much going on that Noah employed the escaped former slaves who could speak the language to organise it all while he met with the representatives of the various guilds.

People who live in cities or in caves have one thing in common, where was the next meal coming from? Noah accompanied by two Tufek took the guild heads to view the store of food, the results were not good. The store of food would not last more than a few days. As yet there was no word from the forest. Would they be willing to feed their former enemy?

The next morning, the fourth day, Barry, Sam and Jim along with three Tufek went hunting. This time they rode north out of the city in search of herd animals, late in the afternoon they returned with nothing to report.

Noah said to Jock, "The drought has driven them away. Perhaps they will come back now that the rain has returned." Jock's 'hope so' lacked enthusiasm.

Junior said, "The plain's animals that migrate to our plain must give this city of Geyin a wide berth."

In the evening in one of the houses that the clans now called home, the talk was still of going home. Everyone seemed to agree except Jock but he wouldn't rebuke any dissention. "OK, if we can't go home, what do we do?" said Barry.

Noah said, "I've been talking to the guilds and asked them apart from food and water, what was needed most to get the city running again and it's wood."

Noah continued, "It seems wood for the fires are the next most important thing, the drought and cutting trees has made this land bare. They also say the remaining grain or some of it be protected, and kept for planting next year.

"They have examined the food in the big house and there isn't enough for everyone. The people were starving before we arrived and it seems despite our efforts, things are going to get worse."

That night as Jock tried to sleep, he thought maybe everyone is right. Maybe we should go home and just leave the Adnin to their own resources. Then he remembered it was getting too late in the year to go home. They would have to stay in the city until spring.

The next morning on their fifth day, he awoke, and had made a decision. Two men despite the late summer or early autumn would go back to the clan and tell them what had happened. He chose Junior and Jude and as an after-thought Mia, she didn't want to go but when she was reminded that her father Charlie was with the clan, she at once changed her mind.

The next day, Jock decided that there should be another hunt this time with more resources. Five clan and five Tufek rode east, the dry earth had soaked up the recent rain making the riding easy and in less than half a day, they came to a wooded hillside with plenty of dry wood. Deer could be seen running and hiding. High in the branches, swinging from tree to tree were what the

Tufek called monkeys and they assured the clansmen that they were good to eat.

Barry didn't think there would be enough animals in the woods to sustain the city but it all helped and with the travois to transport game and wood, starvation could be put off for a little longer.

With their blowpipes, the forest people brought down six monkeys. It wasn't much, but it was the only fresh meat that the city had seen for many moons.

The next day, led by Barry more horses, men and travois left for the only known source of wood and game that they knew. Before evening, they returned loaded with wood three small deer and more than ten monkeys.

That evening Jock questioned Barry about the day. He said, "There's plenty of wood but the easy picking will not last, even with their metal swords we will end up trying to cut down the bigger trees and I don't think there is many animals, it's not a very big wood. In the distance, we saw a range of hills maybe a day's journey. Maybe we will have more luck there."

The next morning, the food situation was becoming critical. Jock decided that every horseman and travois that could be spared and some of the younger fitter citizens would leave to explore the hills that Barry had seen. There was little spare food. If the explorers didn't find anything, they would return hungry.

The clan had arrived with ten, ten and two horses. Davy of the Tufek, the escaped slave along with Barny, Terry and Becks had taken ten to the forest.

Jock, Junior and Jude stayed in the city. The remaining clan, Barry, Jim, Sam and Buddy aided by eight former Tufek escaped slaves and a few of the fitter Adnin and the remaining ten and two horses each towing two travois left in the early light of a late summer morning.

Progress was slow because of the men on foot. Barry decided to press on with the horsemen leaving the men on foot to follow as best they could.

The clan and Tufek horsemen reached the foothills by mid-afternoon. As they approached, Sam observed, "Not as high as our home hills." He turned and looked north and south. "Although maybe as long as our hills, I wish that is where I was right now." No one argued with him.

They reached the tree line, set up camp, then separated to explore the hills. Jim decided to go over the top of the smallest to see what was on the other side and his news was good and on meeting Barry, he said, "I believe the plain on the other side is the path that the herd animals take in autumn and spring and I don't think it's too late in the year to hunt them as they pass to their winter quarters."

There was other good news. Buddy found a tarn, a small lake half way up on one of the higher hills. There were animal tracks everywhere.

The Tufek horsemen had tended to stay together and when they came back, they were excited but with no one to translate their news was slow in coming until they stopped jabbering in their language and raised all their hands with ten fingers extended and then pointed to their horses. It was obvious they had seen a herd of horses.

Everyone got excited, Barry kept a cool head and said to Sam, "Take Buddy, spread out and find the men on foot, guide them into camp. Jim and I will go and find some horses."

Sam and Buddy would have rather gone in search of horses but obligingly they mounted up, swung round and headed west.

Tufek leading the way, Barry and Jim followed. They turned north before riding uphill into a sparsely tree lined wood. Shortly, the hill started to flatten out. The Tufek dismounted, tied their horses and moved quietly forward with Barry and Jim following behind. As they moved forward, the trees became even more sparse.

They stopped and looked through the last of the trees onto a large plateau, many tens of ten paces in size and in it grazing quietly was a herd of about ten and ten and another ten of horses. The stallion was easy to spot, bigger than the rest. He was the only horse with his head up and not grazing. He sniffed the air and looked suspiciously to where the men lay but took no action. Barry indicated withdrawal and slowly everyone backed off to their own horses who were agitated being able to smell the herd.

Barry led men and horses further downhill before tying them up again.

"Did you see the rock face at the far end of the plateau? It had a split, an opening, a canyon with a stream running out of it."

Jim agreed and said, "We need to find out if that canyon is big enough and if there is another way out."

Leaving two of the forest people with the horses, Barry and Sam took the rest, they split up with Barry heading south and Jim heading north, both giving the plateau a wide berth. The plan was to try to get above the cliff face and explore the canyon from the cliff top.

* * * *

It was nearly dark when the two groups emerged on top of the cliff and silently waved to each other across the canyon. It was as perfect as it could get, it was indeed a blind and at the far end, water cascaded down a rock face into a pool before running out into the stream they had seen earlier. Barry estimated that the canyon opened out to a width of at least ten and another ten and another ten paces. More than enough space to corral the whole herd if they only they could drive the herd into the canyon.

Waving goodbye, the two groups returned to their horses by the same route, retrieved their horses and headed to the camp, reaching it after dark. The men on foot had arrived only shortly before them.

That night, there was barely a mouthful of meat for each man and before settling down for the night, it was agreed that the horses were the number one priority.

The stars shone brightly. It turned cold, too early for frosts but they were not far away. The next day promised to be eventful.

Lying on hard ground, Barry's furs did little to soften it, sleep didn't come easy. His mind wandered over the events of the day, if they could drive the horses into the canyon, how to keep them there?

As a child, he remembered the time before horses and the great autumn hunts when every man woman and child from all the clans worked together to kill as many animals from a herd as possible as they made their annual migration to more sheltered parts, failure to do so would bring starvation and death.

Chapter Thirty-Two
Horses

The clans would use wood and brush to build walls to funnel animals into the killing zone. The same idea, was going to be used to block the entrance to the canyon.

Next morning, there was only water. The meagre supply of meat was gone. Barry told everyone of his plan.

Sam pointed out, "The trees are a lot thinner near the horses, it might be better to gather wood and brush there."

It was agreed and so the clansmen spread out and brought down fallen wood and brush out from the tree line and dumped them by the camp. Despite the language barrier the rest of the party did the same even if they didn't know why they were doing it. In the end, there was so much material, the travois were fully loaded, the rest carried by the men on foot.

By midday, the Tufek indicated it was time to enter the trees and head uphill. Everyone gratefully deposited their burdens on the ground and waited for instructions from Barry. His plan was similar to the hunts pre-horse, drive the herd to where the clans wanted them to go, in this case into the canyon.

Barry divided everyone into three groups led by Jim, Sam and Buddy, with his own men briefed. They all set off uphill to the field of the horses.

Jim and his men spread out themselves to the south, Sam circled to the north, Buddy waited a time then spread out his men lower down,

Slowly advancing uphill until the trap was complete.

Barry stepped through the last of the trees, took a few steps on to the field and stopped. The stallion spotted him immediately, he had been sniffing the air for some time but did not recognise these new smells as a threat. When Barry stopped walking, this was the signal for everyone to walk out into the open.

Barry raised his arm, immediately everyone started to walk slowly forward while shouting and howling. The mares with half-grown foals immediately ran into the canyon and as the circle of men tightened, the rest of the herd followed, it was easy as that.

The next job was to bring up the brush and wood to make a barrier across the entrance and as an afterthought, Barry ordered fires lit on the field side of the barrier. Meanwhile, Jim took three Tufek up on top of the canyon and pointed out the stallion. Three darts from their blowpipes rendered the animal unconscious, the rest of the herd screamed and moved into the canyon as far as they could.

Sam and Buddy took their horses into the canyon dragged the unconscious stallion out into the field and butchered it.

Two Tufek loaded up their travois with the stallion's meat and headed back to the city.

Barry had a plan but the language problem between clan, Tufek and Adnin was such that the clansmen had to make the decisions and somehow let their plans be made known to the Tufek and the Adnin and not for the first time there was much arm waving, pointing and shouting.

Barry's plan was to send Buddy and all the Tufek and Adnin back to camp, enter the hills near the tarn and bring down as much game as possible. Meanwhile, Barry, Jim and Sam would reinforce the barrier, keep the fires stocked and then climb on the cliff and decide which horses to keep and which horses to slaughter, they were all to meet up at the camp at the end of the day.

Late afternoon, the three men stood on top of the cliff and examined the herd nervously milling around their prison. Jim calculated there were ten, ten, ten and ten of horses and about ten and five of foals.

Three of the stallions looked to be in early adulthood. They would have to go for meat, there were younger stallions not fully grown and mares without foals, their fate was still to be decided.

Back in the field, Barry asked Jim and Sam to guard the entrance to the canyon while he went back to camp with a promise to send help first thing in the morning.

* * * *

When he arrived at the camp, there was no one there, but he was soon joined by the rest of the expedition bringing down from the hill butchered monkeys, deer, even a wild pig so much that the Tufek had run out of darts and instead of two darts per kill, one dart was used to slow, render unconscious or disorient the animal at which point men rushed in for the kill, even climbing trees to dislodge unconscious monkeys.

Butchering their kills ready for transport went on till after dark.

The next morning, Barry made a slight change to his plan. He sent Buddy and five Adnin and supplies up to Jim and Sam with a promise that re-enforcements with as much rope as could be found sent back as soon as possible. Meanwhile, everyone else headed for the city of Geyin as quickly as possible.

Chapter Thirty-Three
A Journey Home

Junior, Jude and Mia had only been travelling for a few days. Progress was good, the drought had dried the land. Junior with that terrific memory of his people and along with Jude, recognised landmarks and the best route to take to avoid bad ground. They were hopeful of reaching home before the worst of winter.

* * * *

When Barry and the rest of party arrived, the city was abuzz with excitement; just the day before a long column of men and horses arrived coming from the west. The column led by Barny, Terry, Becks and the former slave Davy followed by a long line of the Tufek led by their main headman Hugh.

Each horse was dragging two travois filled to overload with meat and fruit, a line of Tufek carried baskets of more fruit and meat.

It was getting dark when the head of the column stopped in front of the great palace of Rufus, the tail filling the plaza at the bottom of the hill. Davy re-introduced Hugh to Jock who before giving Hugh the guided tour of the palace, ordered that a large guard be mounted to protect the food. It was not necessary as the

Tufek had already started to gather their loads together and had no intension of allowing hungry Adnin near.

Hugh's tour of the palace wasn't made in the dark. Hundreds of candles had been lit in the great hall and in the upper rooms. As Hugh and his entourage entered, the more stolid headman appeared unimpressed. Not so his companions, their cries and gasps needed no explanation.

This was the first time since their arrival that clansmen had seen all the candles lit. The light impressed Jock and like Hugh, he kept his own council.

The Tufeks born in a forest stood in wonder at the huge enclosed space. They touched the smooth walls, gazed at the alcoves with the many wonderful statuettes and ceramics and would have wandered further before Jock guided Hugh and his entourage up the stairs and into the living quarters of the late Rufus and his high priests.

The tour ended up in the banqueting hall where Jock guided Hugh to a seat at the great table. Hugh was less impressed with the table than Jock had been. In the world of the clans, tables did not exist but the Tufek in their long huts had built and used tables always.

Hugh spoke to one of his men and shortly a stream of men carrying baskets of food were on the great table, and as they ate, like people everywhere, small talk started until, through Davy, Jock asked, "These people were your enemy. They killed your people and enslaved them, why are you being so generous."

Hugh replied, "Davy tells me we don't need to worry about them any longer. Thanks to you, they can no longer harm us."

Davy spoke, "Although we live in the forest and we always will, there is no reason why we can't look beyond it. These horses of yours are a wonder. Hugh thinks that if we could have some, we could explore into the great plain."

Jock did not say anything. His horses were too precious to give away, but these people were allies, he knew he would have to do something.

By now, it was dark. Eight-thousand years ago when darkness fell, no matter who you were, you turned in for the night.

In Rufus's great house, despite the myriad of candles, that's what everyone did.

The next morning, hundreds of hungry citizens were up and milling about. The Tufek who had been up all night guarding the food were not in a mood to distribute it. The crowd was starting to get ugly. It was then that Barry and his men arrived. They entered the city coming in from the east and arrived first, at the palace, and then confronted by chaos, the citizens were becoming hostile and impatient.

Jock standing on the top of the steps would have loved to run down and greet Barry and his men, but the scene was getting out of control. The Adnin outnumbered the clan and Tufek many times over and in all sides, they were starting to press in to the supplies brought in by the forest people.

Jock with his panoramic view at the top of the steps saw the danger. He shouted to Barry, "Drop your loads, use the horses to move these people back. If you have to use your sticks and swords, use them."

Barry seeing the situation, did as commanded and split clan and Tufek horseman in two and walked forward driving a wedge between food and citizens. This did not go down well. Some hotheads in the crowd, unused to horses and not appreciating their power, tried punching the animals on their head or flanks. The Tufek riders, who already had no love for the Adnin, reacted instantly. Swords and sticks rained down on the citizens.

clan horsemen much more experienced, used their mounts to swerve and swipe driving citizens away from the besieged Tufek. Then the worst happened, a knife was drawn, a rider was stabbed in the leg, further down the line, a horse was slashed in the flank. This time a rider didn't use the flat of his sword to move the people, this time blood ran on to the flags. It took only seconds for the crowd to see what was happening. As one they turned and fled.

The Tufek guards stood impassively, the horsemen dismounted and examined the wounded citizens.

Noah said to Jock, "I'll go and round up the heads of the guilds and bring them here."

As he rode down the avenue, Jock told Barry, "Take two men and protect Noah. This is the city's problem. And one more thing, tell Noah to pass the word; no one gets fed today."

* * * *

Jock turned to Barry and heard all his news; his first thoughts flew back to his talk with Hugh. His pool of horses could not be spared. But with luck the wild horses found by Barry was just what was needed.

Noah came back before midday with the heads of the city guilds, by then their friends had removed the wounded. The guilds were assembled at the bottom of the steps and addressed by Jock.

"While there is food and fuel, we will feed you. But know this, the people of this city will assemble in the square at the bottom of the avenue and are not permitted to come up to the palace to collect food until directed by you and even then you will marshal them up at no more than three ten of tens at once."

Noah, who was translating for Jock, changed three tens to thirty citizens.

* * * *

Buddy, Jim and Sam back with the corralled horses needed help as soon as possible and when Jock realised the situation and the potential of a supply of horses, he organised a third bigger expedition to relieve them, every scrap of rope was commandeered.

Barry had no choice but to lead this new mission to bring horses to the city. Jock said to Hugh, "We just might be able to give you the horses you wanted."

The next morning as every horse and rider available were about to start to relieve the clansmen guarding the captured horses when Jock made a slight change of the plan. He detailed five Tufek horsemen to support Noah and Davy as they went down the hill to the square and confront the hungry citizens of Geyin.

Chapter Thirty-Four
Horses and Bison

Autumn started to head to winter, this far south while there were frosts and sometimes snow, compared to the weather further north the climate was much softer.

Barry and his men came back with by Noah's count thirty-five mares, their foals and four young stallions. Stone and wood houses near the plaza were commandeered as stables for all the horses, internal walls knocked down and the animals installed, breaking and training began.

Butchered stallions brought back from the hills, game hunted in the hills and food brought from the forest by the Tufek kept the Adnin from starving but they were always hungry.

Early winter, the weather held. It wasn't cold, Jim approached Jock and said, "Remember I said I went on to the other side of the hills and found the great plain, it might not be too late in the year to hunt the plain's animals."

Jock realised if the plain's animals could be hunted as they migrated south, the city and its citizens might be saved.

That evening Jock reminded everyone of Jim's discovery.

* * * *

Before everyone had turned in for the night, Jock out lined to everyone his plan to try to hunt the plain's animals.

Before first light just as the black of night lightened, the original team Barry, Jim, Sam and Buddy and four forest horsemen left the city and headed east. They were to make best speed, pass through the wood onto the hills where the horses were found and ride beyond the hills and onto the great plain. Jock's plan didn't go beyond that, would there be herds migrating south or were they too late in the year and even if a herd was spotted could anything be done to slaughter some, as Jock said to Jim, "You're in charge, do what you see fit."

Jim and his men came down out of hills two days later and surveyed the all too familiar plain although their forest companions familiar with the confines of their forest were in awe of the huge expanse of land.

The land was barren of any animal life. The men feared that they were too late in the year to find the herds.

Jim said, "No point in going south if the herds have already passed through, we're too late, we should head north for a day maybe two. If we don't meet a herd and make some kills, I am afraid we have failed."

The hunters turned north and within half a day came across a river flowing south although much reduced by the drought.

Buddy speculated, "Is this the river that runs through the city?"

They followed its western bank, the ground gradually rising, and by the time they made camp that evening, the hunters were on a bluff many times the height of a man above the river.

* * * *

A fire lit and almost the last of their dry food eaten, before they settled down in their furs for the night, Sam said, "What now? Do we keep going north?"

Jim stuck to his plan. "One more day, then we turn back."

As the night deepened, it turned cold. Everyone was uncomfortable and awake before dawn, the fire was out with little wood nearby to restart it, almost without words or orders, everyone mounted up and headed north.

Before midday, a cloud of dust was seen on the horizon, it had to be a large herd. If they were driven east towards the high ground above the river and stampeded over the bluff, salvation for the city was at hand.

Not a new concept to the hunters from the clans, and so it happened the herd of bison hemmed by the tree covered hills on their left and confronted by men on horseback in front of them veered east towards the river. As they approached the high ground, more shouting and screaming horsemen stopped their eastward movement. They were now flanked by horsemen on both sides, there was only one way for them to go, to the high ground above the river.

The shouting and screaming horsemen rode right up to the edges of the herd. The animals began to panic, and tried to move into the centre. There was no room, animals being jostled on two sides started to panic and run forward right to the edge of the bluff above the river, the pressure of the animals behind them was too great. One after another with increasing frequency, bison lost their footing and were pushed over the edge.

The day started to draw to an end there were hundreds of dead and dying bison at the bottom of the bluff, some lying in the shallow river most on dry land. There was nothing that eight men could do. It would take the manpower of most of the city to recover, process and store this harvest.

Eight horsemen set out the next morning to bring the news to the city.

Jock on receiving the news immediately called Noah who in turn called the heads of the city guilds and after much discussion and interpreting for Jock, plans made. It would be a huge undertaking, it would take many weeks and would involve many citizens. A village in the woods near the river would have to be built to accommodate all the workers, cooking facilities, a workshop to maintain metal tools, another workshop to construct the many travois needed, a tannery, a ropery would there be enough horses.

During the evening meal Jock said, "If they want to eat, we'll stand aside and let them get on with it."

Part Five

Chapter Thirty-Five
Nearly Home

Junior, Jude and Mia had now been travelling for more than ten days and were more than half way home. They had skirted the horror of the massacred Adnin army and were making good progress. Junior was not sure, he thought thanks to horses they could be home in another ten days.

* * * *

Miles to the north, the village below the former Mizuki caves was all but complete, a start had been on wood and mud walls to help protect the huts from the worst of the winter weather.

Everyone took it for granted that a hunt would be successful, no one went hungry.

Tentative efforts made to plant tubers and edible roots on the plain near the village and rudimentary fields were appearing. Charlie oversaw this work and enjoyed his raised status. He had gone from a headman to a slave and back to a man of knowledge and status. He also advised on the cutting and drying of the flax grasses, although it was too early to think about weaving.

Mike was starting to feel his age. If he thought about it, the people were healthier and therefore living longer. He started to think of who would be his successor.

His deputies, former clan leaders in themselves, Ash, Murph and Star were fine subordinates. But, of an age with him and besides frankly, he didn't think anyone of them would be up to the job, there was only one man in his opinion up to the job and that was Junior. He hoped that he would return from the expedition to the south safely.

Much of the pressures of surviving had eased. Mike had the time to watch Fred's successors, Luke and Ben, and was gratified that they were turning out to be worthy successors to that great man.

Fred's ambition was to produce a replica of the Moyan clan's lonesome pine on the plain below the village. This time not in wood but in stone.

With Mike, it had become an obsession. A start had been made, not without much moaning and gnashing of teeth from the men roped into felling trees for logs for rollers to digging out a suitable splinter of granite fallen from a tor to dragging it on log rollers to a large hole, its position decided by two fresh-faced youths soon to be men.

* * * *

Mike's plan for a new lonesome pine made from stone took a lot of manpower, but the lives of the people in the last few years had changed dramatically, they were no longer living on the edge, people had more time to follow other pursuits and Mike channelled that energy into his obsession.

Fred's replacement granite lonesome pine was finally installed, but before further work in installing smaller stone markers to follow the sun as it moved in the heavens throughout the year, the weather turned wet and cold.

Mike thought of continuing the boys' plan despite the weather, but common sense prevailed. The north facing walls needed to be enforced. Ash, that expert in all things in the construction of huts and tents, along with men from his clan started inspections and recommendations to improve the people's living quarters. Materials found and prepared to implement his recommendations and once again, the village was abuzz with activity.

Further south, Junior, Jude and Mia continued heading for home, the weather turned colder as they moved north. Junior was becoming worried that they might not reach home before the real winter hit. If an early snowstorm caught them on the exposed great plain, their chances of survival would be poor.

He missed Sasha and his mum. Did he have a child? If he did, he hoped it would be a boy.

The weather closed in, cold rain driving wind, low clouds blotted out the sky. With heads down, they continued for two days. The horses were exhausted. They were cold, wet and exhausted. They had to find shelter. If they did not and the weather kept up or got worse, they knew that they would die here out on the great plain.

Mid-afternoon on the second day, it was already starting to get dark.

Jude spotted a large tor barely visible through the murk and rain. He pointed east to the tor and without a word, all turned and headed for it and the hope of shelter.

Junior was cold, wet and tired. If he hadn't been, he would be overjoyed. He would have recognised the tor, it was no more than a day from home and more importantly, it had a large south facing overhang offering shelter.

Horses and humans crowded into the overhang and out of the rain and endured a cold wet night with the heat from everyone's bodies gradually taking out the killer cold.

Hours later, Jude said, "I think the heat from our horses' bodies has probably saved our lives."

Gradually as the night progressed, the rain and wind lessened and in the morning, the nearness of home spurred everyone on. The party left without eating any of the meagre supply of food.

Junior looked west and as the clouds cleared, there to him was that wonderful place, the escarpment and home.

Tired and exhausted, they plodded on unaware of a hunting party led by Robin. They were looking for stragglers from the great herds now well on their way to more sheltered areas further south.

Stragglers had become easy pickings at this time. They consisted of females with late, undernourished or lame calves and older animals unable to keep up with the herd.

The hunters continued south and east and in the distance and in the mist, they could see men and horses obviously heading towards the escarpment. The hunters immediately turned and headed towards them. As they got closer, the riders appeared not to have noticed them. They were barely in control of their horses. Heads down, the horses were in charge as they plodded towards home.

Robin shouted at them. The riders didn't appear to notice even their horses ignored the hunters as they approached. It took Robin to stop in front of the lead horse to get their attention. The lead horse with his way blocked was forced to stop. Junior lifted his head and re-joined the clan.

The riders from the south were too tired, cold and exhausted. They barley acknowledged their saviours. Robin remembered when he was in the party carrying supplies to the whole Vornay nation as they made their slow, painful way across the great plain. He took charge and gently lifted Junior from his horse.

The riders were in trouble, they were at their lowest ebb. Robin doubted that if they hadn't been found, men and horses may well have died on that great plain and within sight of salvation.

The hunters grabbed and held all three to try to give them some of their body heat.

Robin gently started to disrobe Junior, and with another hunter holding him upright, dressed him in what spare clothing was available. Even to the extent of taking off some of his own to cover an almost comatose Junior. As Robin gently laid him down, he was minded of a long time ago when a little Vornay girl offered him to hold in his arms a new born Lamb.

On the plain, the only source of heat was body heat. While Junior, Jude and Mia were, dressed and supported by the hunters, Robin sent a rider of to the clan with the news that Junior, Jude and an unknown female were in urgent need of help less than half a day from the clan.

Mike, on hearing the news immediately started to organise a relief column and in the close-knit community of clan and Vornay, the return of two of their sons known to everyone. Mike was inundated with volunteers wanting to go to their aid.

A much-revived Junior, Jude and Mia would arrive in the clans' meeting place just before dark. Despite the cold, the place was crowded, fires had been lit, women had brought food, everyone was excited. Here were men known to all, arriving back from an exciting and dangerous mission.

Rumours spread like wildfire. Where was the rest of the party? What had happened to them? Were they alive? If they were, where were they and who was the mysterious woman who was never far from Jude's side.

Eventually, a long column of horses and men made their way up the path to the meeting place. Men dismounted, boys ran forward and led the horses away. The group stood hesitantly at the edge of the space, the silence was overpowering. Robin pushed his men back and pushed the three heroes forward towards the leaders' hut, they were not even halfway there when the former slave Charlie let out a yell and rushed forward, "Mia, Mia, Mia, my daughter."

Buster shouted, Lilly screamed, they rushed forward to greet their son Jude.

Junior, for a few moments, stood alone until Sasha pushed her way out of the crowd and rushed forward with her new-born son.

In that moment, Mike knew that the party he had sent out to find and observe the monsters were safe.

It was some time before things settled down everyone was hugging everyone. Junior couldn't take his eyes off Sasha and his son. Mike broke up the happy reunion.

"Everyone is desperate to know what has been happening. Junior, Jude, you need to stand up here and now and tell us all of what has been happening."

Thousands of years ago long before books, newspapers, semaphore the telegraph, radio, television, computers, the Internet, tablets and smart phones, people were hungry for anything out of the ordinary and more so for news. People of the clans and the Vornay were no less intelligent than we are today, they just lacked the where for all to satisfy that need and in reality, didn't even know that they had a need, but tonight that need would be more than satisfied.

In front of the leaders' house, Junior and Jude disentangled themselves from their loved ones, took a few steps forward, stopped and looked out at the huge crowd, the murmur subsided to complete silence.

Junior, ever the showman, spoke first, "We left here in the very early spring, we were instructed by Mike to seek and find the monsters who killed the Mizuki clan and the Fox family. This we did, not only did we find them, we conquered them." His audience gasped and were further mesmerised, not a sound was heard.

Jude found his voice, "After we left our homes, we travelled south for many days." He turned and gently pulled Mia to the front. "This is Mia, daughter of Charlie. Do you all know Charlie?"

The audience reacted, everyone knew Charlie and let Jude know that they did.

Junior took up the story, "Mia like Charlie was a slave, she escaped from the southern monsters. These monsters have a name and I will tell you that name, they are called the Adnin and they live in a village many, many, many times bigger than our homes on the escarpment."

Every one gasped, few really understood.

Jude continued, "As we travelled south, we met Mia travelling north looking for her father. She had not eaten for days and was very ill."

Junior said, "Jude tended to her and made her better, just look at the way they look at each other."

A bit embarrassed Jude glared at Junior, who went on, "When Mia was better, she told us of many things. There was a great drought, it hadn't rained for many moons, people and slaves in the town were dying. She said there were other people who the Adnin had attacked but had failed to conquer; they lived in a forest."

Jude explained how they met these forest people who called themselves the Tufek and they became allies against the Adnin, he went on to say, "We went into the forest to one of their villages and do you know what they have?" He paused for a few seconds, his audience waited, "They have wolves that are allowed to wander about the village and I have seen with my own eyes children playing with them, and do you know what else they have, they have big birds that can't fly. They lay lots of eggs which make good eating and do you know what, sometimes, they kill a bird and roast it and Junior will agree with me, the meat of these birds is the best you will ever taste."

This was just too much for the people, everyone was on their feet shouting questions asking for more details. A few didn't believe the fantastic story about birds and wolves but nearly everyone else did.

Mike came forward, stood in front of the group and quietly waited for the hubbub to subside; such was his presence that the hubbub quickly did.

"It's too dark now, this story will have to wait until tomorrow. What I can tell you that those who were left were alive and were in charge of the monsters from the south who we now know are called the Adnin. We will all meet again tomorrow."

The people made their way from the meeting place, most with their heads buzzing.

Chapter Thirty-Six
The City Saved

The city/town of Geyin, the home of the Adnin appeared to be deserted. Large numbers of its citizens and some of the fitter slaves had left to process the bison driven over the cliff, the job was huge and would take at least a moon.

Everyone knew that if the people and their town was to survive, the job had to be completed before winter.

Every day travois of meat and wood arrived in the town. Jock didn't think the stockpile of fuel would be enough to last all winter. He wondered if John of the Tufek could help, their forest was closer and the possibility of a gift of horses might encourage the Tufek to help out with wood and possibly fruit and vegetables. He decided to make the journey himself, all the better for two headmen to conduct negotiations over wood, food and horses. Thus, he and Noah set out for the forest.

The ever-watchful forest natives greeted the two horsemen as they approached the tree line and escorted them into the village. As usual, there were children, tame wolves and birds everywhere. Jock hoped that there would be birds on the upcoming meal. He remembered his one and only taste of these creatures and made a mental note to include them in any negotiations with John. After the formal greetings, there was a meal and to Jock's delight there were birds on the menu.

During the meal and afterwards, Jock with Noah and an escaped Tufek slave conducted halting and much translated negotiations.

It quickly became apparent that John was very interested in horses.

"Can you really ride on the back of one all day long without having to walk?"

Jock put him right, "More or less, on a long journey we need to stop maybe four or five times to give them a short rest. It depends on the load they are carrying and the type of ground and to feed and water them. If we stop by a stream, they can drink and graze by themselves, there is a lot to learn about keeping horses safe and well."

Jock thought now would be the time to talk of gifting some horses to the Forest People.

"All our horses are being used to transport meat and wood to Geyin but that task will be over soon, I think we could spare a few right now and more when their work is finished."

The promise of horses now and more later made talk of Tufek's help for the Adnin easy.

The plan was for Jock, Noah and five Tufek to return. The five Tufek would undergo training in horse welfare and return to the forest as soon as possible. In the meantime, the Tufek would construct enough travois ready to start the transport of food and wood to the town. When the last of the bison meat was stored, more horses would be released to Tufek and more training given.

Jock got his wish; live birds donated to the town.

* * * *

The year rolled on, the nights becoming longer and colder and clear frost formed nearly every night.

Noah said to Jock, "I've never seen it as cold this early."

Jock commented, "Compared to our home, this weather isn't so bad."

The last of the bison meat had arrived, most of it stored in the palace.

The rest in some of the stone houses, which meant more evictions of some of the elite, whose complaints fell on Jock's deaf ears. However, he did notice a distinct lack of urgency about food over the coming winter.

Noah said, "Before the drought, there always seemed to be enough grain and meat was stored as we are doing now and there were animals to slaughter when necessary."

One cold frosty morning, the clear sky started to cloud over with the wind picking up. By evening, it started to snow and before long it was a full-blown blizzard and by morning the wind and snow kept the good citizens of Geyin indoors. There was, however, movement in the town. The men from the north, Jock, Jim, Barry, Sam, Barny, Terry, Beks, Buddy and a reluctant ex-slave from the south, Noah ventured out into the storm, horses had to be fed and watered in their stone-built stables. However, some of the less fortunate citizens lived in hovels a lot meaner than clans' new village on the escarpment many miles to the north. Barny, Terry and Beks went down the hill to see how the poorer people of Geyin had faired and they hadn't fared well.

The unusual wind and snow this far south had collapsed many of their homes.

Barny, Becks and Terry found people cowering in what shelter their former homes offered.

Barny said, "I don't understand these people. Why don't they move to the soldiers' buildings, they look undamaged and are empty. Even the slaves' prison appears undamaged."

It occurred to Barny that the poor of the city only one level up from the slaves, and now one level below them, were too intimidated to think for themselves. So he acted for them and started moving them to the soldiers' quarters and the slaves' quarters, then had to move some of them back outside to their former homes to dismantle anything combustible.

By midmorning, the snow had more or less stopped, although it was hard to tell with gale blowing the snow everywhere.

* * * *

Jock had left the distribution of food to the city guilds, which meant in practice, at midday people gathered outside the great temple to collect their rations for the day.

Jock had said to Becks and Terry, "You be there every day, let the guilds give out the food try and see if it's done fairly, I know this might not be easy but do your best." He had another thought. "Speak to Noah, he speaks the language, ask him to mingle with the crowds and see if he can pick anything up."

The men from the clan idly watched as people started to make their way to collect their food for the day. Terry commented, "They don't seem worried, do you think that they are so used to the rule of the priests and the soldiers and to have slaves doing a lot of the work that they can't see what could happen in a bad winter or another drought?"

Jock snapped his fingers, "Terry, you are right, what is needed here before we go home in the spring is for the people to start doing things for themselves."

Jim said, "They need a clan chief like Mike, not a monster like Rufus."

Barny thought that Noah before he was a slave was the headman of his village and when he speaks to the Adnin, they certainly do as he orders.

Jock thought it would be difficult for a former slave to be their headman and said as much.

Terry said, "It was you that said we can't just go home and leave them to starve and die. Look what you, we've done, we've saved them."

The wind still blowing the snow around, everyone wanted out of the cold and went up the steps into the palace, but their thoughts and their conversation continued. They headed to the room with the great table, which concentrated their thoughts on their stomachs.

They were hungry, although not for long.

In the middle of the day and in the evening, the men of the clan gathered in the room with the great table. And there, they were served and fed by the former slave girls of the last regime, most of them had nowhere else to go and seeing how the clansmen had dealt with their former torturers, felt safer in the palace than in the outside world. Noah took them under his wing and found them employment in the great palace.

* * * *

There can be only one outcome when young men and young women come in close encounter with each other. Jock realised that when they went home, they wouldn't be alone.

The midday meal arrived, Jock watched as the girls served their meal and which girl was making eye contact with which of his men and mentally paired them up.

He had been too busy with other things to notice before. Suddenly, he felt envious. He missed Isla and wished he could go home. He was not the first nor would he be the last to discover leadership was a lonely profession.

There and then, Jock decided to do something about it. There were more servant girls than clansmen, why not join his men. He thought of Isla, he missed her but she was not here.

In his mind, he noticed one of the girls didn't appear to be paired with any of his men. She was tall for a female, pretty, fair-haired unlike the other girls, who were dark. Fair hair was common in the clans, to his men darker haired girls were more exotic.

Jock called her over and asked for more water, she bobbed her head and backed off bumping in to one of the other girls. Terry laughed, "She's frightened of you."

Jock didn't understand. "You are the chief, if it wasn't for you, most of the people hereabouts would be dead and they know it. Think of all the things you have done for them; you are more a god king than Rufus ever was."

Jock said, "But you know me, I am no different from any one of you."

Terry said, "We all know that, except that your farts are louder than any of ours, but the people don't know that. I doubt if any of them have ever heard you fart." Everyone was laughing when the water arrived, the girl averted her eyes when she presented the water. Again, she backed away.

Jock quietly said to Terry, "Find out her name."

Chapter Thirty-Seven
Jenny

The conversation on the future of the Adnin after the clan went home continued; Noah was still the most likely leader. Barny said, "We all have dealt with the guilds, most of them are ordinary workers not like the fancy people who lived near the palace. Where are they by the way, I don't see them about these days?"

Jock made a mental note to ask Noah about them.

Barny continued, "Noah could be the chief and work with the guild leaders to run the city when we go home." No one had a better idea than that and so the midday meal broke up.

Jobs needed doing, horses needed attending to and the Forest people in the city needed more training in horsemanship and horse welfare.

A visit was to be made to the food store in the palace.

Jock sought out Terry, "Did you find the girl's name?"

"Her name is Jenny and she belongs to the same clan as Noah." Jock went in search of him and found him deep in the former prison cells below the palace now used as food storage. He was talking to two men from the guilds and was bemoaning the scarcity of salt.

When the men saw Jock, they made their excuses and left. Noah asked if he was looking for him.

"Yes." Then he went on to explain ideas about who should lead the Adnin when the clan went home in the spring.

Noah had been the leader of his clan, now decimated by the Adnin. Surprisingly, he bore no ill will to the people as he said, "Thanks to you, all the real monsters are dead."

In principal, Noah agreed to be the leader but wanted to pick from the guilds the men he wanted to be his lieutenants. Jock agreed and asked if a start could be made soon, he wanted to see how the new administration was working before returning home.

He was about to go when a thought occurred and he said, "What happened to the citizens we evicted who lived in the stone houses near the palace?"

"They moved further down the hill. I've heard that some people were thrown out of their huts to make room for them, I've been meaning to speak to you for some time. I think before you go you will need to train up some citizens to keep order, maybe start a new guild."

Jock started to walk back up the stairs, stopped, turned around, "The girl, Jenny, she was in your clan? What's she like?"

"Why? Do you find her pretty?"

Jock said, "Yes, I do."

Noah laughed, "Well, tell her so."

"I wouldn't know where to start," a rather embarrassed Jock replied.

Noah laughed again, "You are the chief of all the people, you killed many priests, you saved the city and you're frightened to talk to a former slave girl! I can tell you she is friendly, quiet and like most of the girls round here, admire you from afar. Jock, I'll tell her to expect you, just find a reason to speak to her."

A chastened Jock continued up the steps.

* * * *

Late afternoon, the wind increased to a gale. In every building, the shrieking, howling and whistling was deafening. Then, the snow started again, it came down in horizontal sheets, no one ventured out. The storm lasted two days then died suddenly, the wind died completely and over the next ten days the frost was the most severe the city had ever seen. The cold led to deaths among the old and the young, the piles of snow froze solid, people were trapped in their houses and huts.

Only men of the clan, more used to winter weather dared go outside. They immediately started to move families from ruined huts to the stone-built stables. Barny remembered that the Vornay moved their animals into their tents in the worst of the winter storms. The families at first were reluctant, but soon appreciated central heating provided by the horses.

The worst winter in living memory continued, almost continuous confinement in the palace led to liaisons between the men of the clan and their servant girls, the former quarters of the priests were now in good use.

Jock on the other hand was making little progress with Jenny when they met. They seemed tongue-tied.

The cold affected everyone, the only two rooms in the palace with a fire was the kitchen and the huge eating room with the massive table.

As a result, these rooms were nearly always crowded with bored people. One afternoon, the crowd was particularly noisy. Jock went down to balcony seeking peace and quiet, like-minded Noah with him. It was cold but both men were enjoying the peace and quiet and as men do, started putting the world to rights, as men do. Jenny came up the stairs from the food store carrying a basket of food mainly meat.

Noah winked at Jock, "Now's your chance."

As Jenny approached, Noah said, "Here, that basket looks heavy, let me take it upstairs for you. Besides, Jock has something to say to you, stay and chat for a while."

With that, he took the basket and headed upstairs.

Jock looked at Jenny. She looked at Jock, his face and neck became quite red, inanely he almost stuttered. "Noah and you came from the same village. Did you know him there?"

"Everyone knew everyone."

Silence followed. Noah appeared from the bottom of the stairs he had heard every word.

"What a pair of fools you two are. Jock, do you like Jenny?"

"Yes, I do."

"Jenny, do you like Jock?"

"Yes, I do."

Noah sighed, "Jock, take the girl in your arms and at least give her a hug."

* * * *

The winter wore on. In good days, horse and travois went west to scavenge for wood, not a difficult task, storm damage at the edge of the forest was enormous.

Jock and Noah went with the first teams but wanting to see how the Tufek were faring, went deeper in and soon got lost, only to be found hours later by some Tufek fishermen heading for the river, one of them took them back to the village.

The exceptionally cold winter was having an effect on the Tufek but nothing like the hardship endured in the city. The forest gave them protection from the worst of the storms, but for the first time in living memory, snow blanketed the villages.

The fishermen escorted Jock and Noah into the village. Hugh came out to greet them. Jock said, "We just came to see how you were getting on with these terrible storms."

Hugh laughed, "No, you didn't. You came because you wanted to eat some more of our chickens."

Both men laughed. Hugh said, "Come, let's see what we can do for you."

Once again, Jock was overwhelmed by the taste of chicken.

During the meal, he said to Hugh, "Your men and your horses will be able to come back to you when the weather improves. They are as good with them as they ever will be."

Hugh was gratified, "When they come back, why don't you send one of your men to learn about chickens and indeed how to tame wolves?"

Gradually as the year moved on, the weather modified. There was still snow, there were still frosts but as the days went by, the things in the city were becoming easier.

Jock was becoming more relaxed in Jenny's company. He no longer felt that his men were looking at him when he talked to her.

One afternoon after the midday meal was over, some of the girls made it obvious they were heading up to the former priests' sleeping quarters. Terry and the rest of his men started heading in the same direction. Barny the last to leave, he walked out turned came back to Jock, "The room at the end is free, we have put plenty of furs in it for you, all you need to do is go to Jenny and take her there."

Jock did just that. He found Jenny in the kitchen, took her by the hand and led her to the free room at the end of the passage. It was cold but one corner was covered with furs, one piled on top of another.

The priests had forced Jenny into sexual activity on many occasions. She was only alive because she had never become pregnant. She knew what to expect or thought she did. She took her clothes off and slipped under the furs before Jock could do or say anything.

It had been a long time since Jock had held his lovely Isla in his arms, but there is a saying, "A standing cock knows no conscience."

Stripped, Jock joined Jenny under the furs and held her in his arms.

Jenny lay rigid. The least she hoped for was not to be beaten, instead Jock kissed her on the forehead, her nose, her lips and her throat. His tongue slipped down to her breast and circled her areola first, her left and then her right then back to her left. Jenny sank deeper onto the furs.

His hands slipped down to her vagina and then up to her clitoris gently massaging it, he moved his tongue to her nipples. Jenny shuddered.

Moving down her body with his tongue, he stopped briefly at her belly button before moving on to her labia, which he licked and sucked each one in turn.

Slowly, he moved his tongue to her clitoris and using two fingers he pulled skin back to expose as much of the clitoris as possible. Slowly at first, he used his tongue to stimulate her and as Jenny responded, his tongue became faster and stronger.

Finally, Jenny cried out in orgasm, Jock immediately changed position and mounted her. As his penis penetrated, her orgasm continued on and on.

In just a few seconds, both man and the woman were spent and lay quietly in each other's arms. But not so the occupants of the palace. The normally crowded and noisy kitchen and eating room could not but hear their lovemaking. Barny said to the audience. "Please, please, don't let him fart." The joke was lost on everyone except the men of the clan who roared.

Jock and Jenny in modern parlance were now an item, but had little time for each other. As the weather improved, the men of the clan were continually busy. Citizens needed training in horsemanship, further training in hunting was required. It would be some time before the remaining domestic animals were bred in sufficient numbers to sustain the populace.

The guilds at Noah's insistence were becoming increasingly involved, some of their skills were beyond that of the clan, and something not lost on Jock.

There was still the problem of the elite citizens. For months they had blended into the community, but Jock suspected that once the clan went home, they might try to get their old lifestyle back as superior to the rest of the populace.

Jock didn't have an answer. Noah did, "We've discussed this before, we need a new guild, not soldiers but a guild of men who can keep order and answer to the people of the city."

Jock's reply was, "You mean answer to you."

"Yes, but as the leader of the Adnin, I will need people to keep the peace."

Jock left Noah as usual to sort out the details.

Chapter Thirty-Eight
Mike Makes a Decision

On the escarpment, like the city, winter wore on, only so much could be done when the weather closed in. Animals needed to be cared for, extra firewood had to be collected, repairs to huts and walls made. Food distributed.

Mike called on his deputies; Ash, Murph and Star. They all sat down in the meeting hut. There was a fire going but like everywhere else in the village, draughts seemed to take the heat out of fire.

Mike was reluctant to bring what was on his mind. "I am starting to feel the years; you must feel the same."

Star said, "Sometimes when I get up in the morning, I am so stiff, it takes a while before I can walk properly." Ash and Murph agreed. They too had various aches and pains, which made the next part easier.

"I've been thinking who will follow me and be the next leader of our people?" All three men avoided Mike's gaze, it was obvious that none of them wanted the job. As his deputies for too long, they had all the rank and privileges and few of the responsibilities. Nevertheless, he had always appreciated their loyalty and advice.

After a pause, Mike came right out with it, "What do you think of Junior as the new leader?" His friends met his plan almost with relief.

Mike turned his attention to the remaining clan in the city.

"They will be coming home in the spring, let's ask Junior and Jude what they think."

Mike sent for them and on arrival he said, "When do you think Jock will head home, will he return as soon as spring arrives?"

Junior thought and said, "I don't think so, there will be things to see to before they head home."

Jude agreed.

Addressing both of them Mike said, "I think that we should send out another party as early as possible. Hopefully they will arrive before Jock leaves. Will you two start thinking on who should be sent?"

Both men got up to leave, Mike called Junior back. "There is something else, sit back down."

He sat back down and looked warily at the four men. Again, Mike came right out and said, "Junior, we think that you should be the new leader of the people."

Junior was shocked and initially speechless. He had always thought that his late dad would become the next leader as did most people.

"Can I suggest someone else; Jock has been running Geyin in the most difficult circumstances, he is good at it and everyone likes and respects him." He continued, "Besides, I want to continue my father's work, Luke and Ben have come up with some great ideas."

Star said, "What ideas, we already know when summer and winter turns."

"Yes," said Junior, "but right now we don't, for instance, know midsummer's day until the next day when the shadow starts to lengthen, provided there are no clouds, we think we will be able to tell you days in advance when midsummer's day will arrive and over

253

time, we can be more accurate when the animals migrate."

Mike saw the sense in that and called a halt for the day.

Chapter Thirty-Nine
Third Expedition South

The winter wore on, Luke and Ben announced that the year had turned. The people of clan in themselves always seemed to be cold despite their new protection of walls and the many layers of hide covering their tents, almost huts.

The weather was cold and dry with very little wind. Gradually, daylight increased over the long nights. Junior and Jude tasked to mount another expedition south met to select volunteers. They were; Alan, Duke, Nat, Benny, Adam and Brian.

The plan was the expedition heading South would try to meet up with Jock and his men returning home. They headed for the Sleeping Hunter, that great tor, almost a mountain. There they would wait or scout south in the hope of meeting with Jock.

In the meantime, as the winter receded in the city, everyone prepared to go home, excitement mounted at the prospect. Jock realised there were problems on the horizon not least of all Jenny, who was pregnant as were some of ex-slave girls. The original eleven, who had set out from home seemingly such a long time ago, would not be alone as they headed North.

As the weather improved, Jock, making his preparations, thought of all the things that he had seen. He sent for Noah, the ever-busy former slave and now headman of a large town, nearly a city, who arrived eventually.

The two men sat down on the steps in front of the great palace. Jock looked down at the avenue, to the fine buildings and compared them to his home.

He said to Noah, "You know, we will be leaving soon, you'll be in charge, we won't be here, can you cope?"

Noah sighed, "I think so, all the guilds will support me. In fact, they are appreciating their new-found power."

Jock said, "Here's a thought, if you talk to all the guild heads and ask them to nominate a few of their apprentices, let them understand that if there is trouble by the former soldiers and lesser priests, they will be called upon to come to you for direction."

Noah: "You asking me to start an army?"

"No, but the more I think about it, you will need support, you're the leader of the Adnin. Mike is the leader of all the clans but he relies on the other clan chiefs for help.

"I think you'll need help; will the leaders of the Guild give you help and advice or are they too busy with their own guilds to find time to help run the city?"

Noah's thoughtful reply was: "Good question, I think they will help and there is always up and coming young blood in the guilds to help run things. Leave it with me, I will sort something out."

The two men got up to leave. Jock said, "Another thought, could you find some men from the guilds willing to come home with us and teach us your ways?"

"There must be some young bucks with a thirst for adventure." Noah laughed, "Again, I say leave it with me."

Preparations for the clan's now triumphant return home started in the city especially Jock's was such that there was no shortage of young volunteers from the guilds, eager for adventure.

Likewise, John of the Tufek saw advantages in closer co-operation with these warriors from the North. To that end, he arranged for five 'volunteers' to join the northerners on their journey home.

On a bright spring morning, ten clansmen; their women former slaves, some pregnant, some with babies, accompanied with five young guilds men and five Tufek along with five of the forest people, small wolves and wicker cages full of chickens. Jock hoped food would last the journey, it would be a pity to eat the chickens before arriving home.

The city could only spare twenty horses, each horse towing a travois loaded with supplies for the journey.

Noah and half the city turned out to see them off.

The trek would be slow, everyone spent most of the time walking, occasionally a tired and pregnant woman was allowed to ride. Jock's plan was to head towards the remains of the Adnin army, skip West and head for the Sleeping Hunter, there they would rest the horses for a few days.

Meanwhile Alan, Duke, Nat, Benny, Adam and Brian riding south had arrived at the Sleeping Hunter, it was late in the day and the difficult climb to the top would have to wait until morning. Men and horses settled down for the night.

The morning saw the horses fed, watered and hobbled, and the men setting out for the highest climb of their lives. Standing at the bottom and looking up, they wouldn't even have tried it except that they knew that other clansmen had made the ascent and gained the top, and so, with some trepidation, they started to climb.

The reality of the ascent wasn't so bad, there were plenty of hand and foot holds, until they reached the final ascent to the summit, in front of them, many times the height of a man, was a flat plateau of rock gently sloping upwards to a peak. But between the men and the top, a thin spine of rock in places, just a few hand-breadths wide in some places, and on either side, a sheer drop on both sides. The climbers looking down, felt dizzy at the vertical drop to the plain so far below.

Spurred on by the knowledge others had done it before them, the men on their bellies sometimes with legs dangling over the edge, inched forward to the top, the East wind blowing across the spine made things even more difficult.

Slowly, the clansmen inched forward and finally reached the summit, from there it seemed that they could see the whole world. Duke pointed to the west, "You can see the tree line, when Jock comes, I think he will head for the Hunter, if not, we will be able to see them as they pass."

Alan agreed, "I don't think they will pass east, so let's get down before we're blown off by the wind." No one argued.

The men thought the climb to the summit along the spine was bad, it was worse on the way back down, this time their heads were below their feet. It seemed to take forever but eventually, with long pauses, they left the spine behind and stopped for a rest in a sheltered overhang. Nat said, "You can still see the tree line. I, for one, am not going back up to that summit ever again."

It was agreed, and in pairs, the clansmen kept watch while the rest explored their temporary new home and found not too far away a stream supporting a stand of trees, water and firewood made life almost bearable.

Brian started marking a suitable flat rock to mark the days. He'd just marked his eighth morning when Nat and Benny came scrambling down in the distance, they had spotted a column of horses heading directly for the Hunter.

Horses were unhobbled and as everyone started to move out, Alan introduced a note of caution, "It's bound to be Jock but if it's not, we may have to get out fast."

It was Jock and his men and after much laughter, back slapping and friendly pushing, Jock went round everyone and explained who was who. The small wolves were a sensation, they were used to the trek and wandered round, even passing between horses' legs who just ignored them.

Jock said, "Watch this." He took some dried meat from a pack and whistled, immediately the small wolves raced over to him and without prompting, sat down. He gave each one a piece of meat. Once fed, they lost interest and wandered off. The boys were amazed. Benny said, "If I hadn't seen it with my own eyes, I wouldn't have believed it."

Two days later, everyone set out from the Hunter on the final part of their great journey. Days followed days, until the scenery became familiar, and eventually in the distance, the escarpment and home.

Brian and Nat rode off to tell everyone of their arrival.

The summer camp at the foot of the escarpment was in full flow and as the horses approached, everyone abandoned the village and rushed out to greet the returning heroes, what followed were scenes of joy and confusion.

All the original expedition took their girls to meet their families, the exception was Jock as he was dragged off by Isla to meet his son.

Things quietened down. The Adnin and the Tufek stood quietly, not sure what to do.

Mike asked Ash Murph and Star to take the men to the village and offer them something to eat.

Heavily pregnant Jenny, stood alone. Alan, aware of Jock's predicament, took her to Mike and his wife Ruby, and explained the situation. Mike was grim, he said, "Alan, go to Jock and make sure he tells Isla about what's-her-name, oh yes, Jenny. Stay close by when it's all over, bring him to me."

Later much later, Alan and a reluctant Jock approached, Mike strode out to meet them, he raged, "What were you thinking of? You should have left her there." Jock, ruler of a city, slayer of a priest/king, quaked at Mike's onslaught.

Jenny stood beside Ruby, she saw Jock, her Jock, with head bowed being shouted at by a man, her condition made her tired, frightened and lonely. She wanted nothing more than Jock to come to her, she started to cry.

The men turned and walked towards Ruby and Jenny. Just then, Isla, red-eyed from crying, joined them and walked beside Jock. All three walked forward, for Jenny this was too much, her crying turned to uncontrolled sobbing, Ruby patted her on her back. Isla ran to her, put her arms round her and held her tightly, gently stroking her hair and said, "Come with me, you need to rest."

The two woman, supporting Jenny, walked her towards the village.

Jock's relief was palpable, he took a deep breath to keep his legs from giving way. Mike, the great leader that he was, diverted the situation, "Jock, come and show me the small wolves that everyone is talking about."

The two men strolled towards the clans' summer village. "And what about these chickens that Junior was on about, you can show me them as well, is it true that you can eat their eggs?"

Jock replied, "Yes, it's true."

"It looks like things are going to change round here." Mike offered and as the two men reached the centre of the village, Mike said, "I wanted Junior to take my place when I'm gone but he said that you would do a far better job, what do you think?"

Jock said, "Let's see if I can find you an egg."